Convincing

Mr. Northcott

WENDY MAY ANDREWS

CR&O

Sparrow Ink
www.sparrowdeck.com

ISBN - 978-1-989634-46-2

www.wendymayandrews.com

Stay in touch with Wendy May Andrews
and forthcoming publishing news.

Sign up for her biweekly newsletter

Her reputation is on the line. So is his heart...

Gilbert Northcott, second son of the Earl of Everleigh, has no time for frivolity. So, imagine his displeasure when his work as an agent for the Crown forces him to attend a house party. The mission is simple. He is to investigate the one of the wealthy guests. Sadly, the fact that his target's daughter makes him experience actual *feelings* is anything *but* simple...

When Caroline Smith finds out that the handsome Mr. Northcott is investigating her father, she has little choice but to help him. After all, how else can she prove her father's innocence and protect her family's reputation? Falling for the man, however, is *completely* out of the question. He's the very *last* man she could consider suitable marriage material. Or so she keeps telling herself...

Will the truth put this pair of opposites on the path to happily ever after—or tear them apart forever?

Convincing Mr. Northcott, **book 2 in the** *Northcott Kinship* **series, is a light, sweet/clean and wholesome historical romance featuring a smart, strong heroine and the brooding hero who steals her heart. Download today and get ready to fall for Mr. Northcott.**

Dedication

In *Convincing Mr. Northcott* Caroline is trying very hard to make the best of an uncomfortable situation. And then it gets worse. But with determination and perseverance, along with a little bit of love, things end up turning out for the better. This book is dedicated to all those who feel like an outsider. I'm there on the sidelines with you.

XO, Wendy

Acknowledgements

First and foremost, I must acknowledge Mr. Andrews for his constant support of my writing life as well as our non-writing life. I love that he knows Gilbert and Caroline almost as well as I do. Thanks for helping me work out the bugs in the storyline and for taking me for long walks when I needed to get out from behind the screen and for overall dealing with the craziness of living with someone who has so many stories in her head.

My parents, always my biggest fans, enjoy following the adventures of my characters and offer me so much love and support throughout it all. Thank you for a lifetime of that. I couldn't be where I am without you. Thank you too for reading to me as a child. My love of words comes from you.

My beta team, Alfred, Monique, Suzanne, and Christina, are so supportive and helpful in finding any plot holes as well as helping me out all along the way. Thanks so much for your story help as well as your friendship and love!

My gorgeous cover is thanks to the artistry of Envision Literary Photography and Les at GermanCreative. I'm thrilled with my beautiful covers.

My editing team, Bev Rosenbaum and Julie Sherwood, are experts in their field. I am grateful for their input. The characters' goals and motivations have certainly deepened with their help as well as ironing out the kinks in this story, and putting in all the commas that I always leave lying about. Any remaining mistakes are entirely the fault of the author.

Chapter One

Caroline Smith hated being a wallflower. It would never have happened to her back in the village. But here, in Town, even Lady St. John was hard pressed to wash away the stench of her father's money. Caroline supposed it wasn't the money itself that the nobles turned their straight, long noses up about, rather it was his means of acquiring it. It would be much easier for the aristocratic members of Society to accept his largesse if its source were in mines or even shipping. Of course, Roger Smith did have those in abundance, but the problem was his factories. For some odd reason that Caroline could never properly grasp, owning a factory and profiting at it put one nearly beyond the pale.

While she suspected it was jealousy underlying their reactions, Caroline didn't really care what was behind it. She only wished it wasn't the case. Her father had been determined that she take her place in Society. Her "rightful place" as he put it. She supposed as her mother's daughter he wasn't wrong in that assessment. But many of the gentry didn't agree with him. And it was only those who were desperate for her dowry who had thus far taken an interest in courting her. It was most disheartening.

Having perfected the skill of gritting her teeth and smiling pleasantly several weeks ago, Caroline was able to appear as though she were having a pleasant evening even though she wished she were anywhere else at that moment. She had always felt readily able to make friends and feel well-liked, so it had been a hurtful comeuppance to find that wasn't to be the case for her in Town.

With a sigh she glanced around the room. She supposed it would have been easier for the women in the room to accept her if she weren't quite so observable. The shade of her hair was no longer the orange colour she had feared it to be as a child, but it hadn't faded to the honey blonde she had always wished for. And in the bright lights of seemingly a million candles in the crowded ballroom, Caroline feared she appeared as though her head were aglow. Since she was also taller than average, it was impossible for her to hide herself.

Her father would insist no daughter of his ought to ever try to hide herself if he were to know of her feelings on the topic. But Roger Smith would never think to inquire into his daughter's feelings. Not to imply that he would disregard her feelings. He wasn't an absolute lout. In fact, any observer would consider that he was most fond of his daughter. But Caroline was well aware that it was a dreadful disappointment to him that she was a daughter rather than a son who could take over his enterprise from him.

Caroline didn't agree with the assessment that she couldn't take over his enterprise. It was one more thing that she struggled not to resent. Just because she couldn't wear pants didn't mean she couldn't run a business, in her opinion. She had been running through her father's offices and ventures ever since she could toddle. She would like to think she knew them nearly as well as he did. She certainly took an active interest in them, much to Lady St. John's dismay, but still, her father insisted she must marry well. And his opinion of well did not include one of his business associates as Caro would prefer and as she thought would be an intelligent solution to the problem of her being a woman. No, Mr. Smith was quite convinced that his daughter ought to marry a nobleman.

He wanted his daughter to be a lady, he insisted. Caroline was of the opinion that being a true lady had nothing to do with whether or not one had a title but she was hard pressed to convince her father of that truth. Her time amongst the *ton* had done nothing to change her opinion, though. Neither had her father's time changed his, unfortunately. Caro couldn't understand it. The worse the nobles treated Mr. Smith, the more he wanted Caroline to be a part of them. And no amount of arguing had been able to convince the wily old businessman to think how uncomfortable her life would be if they did manage to buy her a noble husband.

"I have been looking all over for you. I should have known you'd be in this particular corner."

Caroline laughed. Daisy was one of the few bright spots about the Society experience. They had met the evening they had both made their curtsy to their monarchs. Caroline had found the act of meeting Queen Charlotte to be both ridiculous and fascinating and had been delighted to make the acquaintance of Miss Daisy Alcott at the same time. She hadn't made many friends while in Town, but she was happy to count Daisy as one of them.

"Why were you looking for me?"

Daisy looked at her as though she had lost her mind. "Need you ask? Lady Fanny."

The name led Caroline to suppress a small shudder. Fanny was one of the many reasons Caroline didn't think being a lady was such a great thing to aspire to.

"Did you wish me to challenge her to a duel on your behalf?" Caro asked with a light giggle, trying to alleviate her friend's obvious discomfort.

Daisy lifted her shoulder in a half-hearted shrug. "I wouldn't mind if you did. Didn't you tell me you were a crack shot?"

Caroline's giggle was genuine this time. "We aren't supposed to say such things aloud, Miss Alcott," she admonished in jest, the laugh sounding through her effort at a scolding tone. "But I'm fairly certain that would put us both firmly outside polite Society."

"Impolite Society, if you ask me," Daisy countered, causing Caroline to snort as she suppressed her laughter.

"Good evening." The deep voice behind her had Caroline stiffening suddenly even as she turned to acknowledge the greeting.

"Mr. Northcott," she replied with a shallow dip while Daisy, ever more polite, dipped down much further. Caroline had to exert a degree of self control to prevent her eyes from rolling in derision. Gilbert Northcott was only the younger son of an earl, not a titled gentleman, certainly not royalty. Caroline couldn't be bothered to subjugate herself in the way her friend seemed comfortable in doing. All the less to the haughty Mr. Northcott.

What does he have to be so haughty about? Caroline couldn't understand the absolute confidence of the man. Yes, he was the most handsome man she had ever seen, but that surely didn't give him license to think he was a superior specimen to anyone else. No doubt, as the son of the Earl of Everleigh and the brother to

Viscount Adelaide, he had influence in certain arenas, but as an untitled gentleman, he really ought not think quite so highly of himself. It wasn't as though he were a doctor or a preacher or some such – someone who could make an actual difference in people's lives.

It ought not make her so angry, but somehow Caroline couldn't quite muster up the discretion she usually exercised in all things. She couldn't explain it, but Gilbert Northcott brought out the worst in her. And she usually was quite adept at avoiding him. But somehow, he had an uncanny ability to seek her out, much like a dog who seemed to sense someone's fear and seek out the most fearful. Caroline rather suspected her antipathy amused him. That fact most decidedly did not amuse her. And so she studiously avoided him whenever possible. But now was not one of those times. She tried not to sigh audibly.

"Are you enjoying your evening?" The corners of his hazel eyes crinkled as he asked the question as though he were secretly amused. If Caroline weren't so put off by his arrogance, she supposed she would like the fact that his eyes crinkled like that even though he wasn't really old enough to have wrinkles. It indicated to her that he laughed a great deal. She was used to everyone around her being too serious, so she thought having a tendency to laugh was an ideal quality. But not if it was at others' expense. And someone as arrogant as Gilbert Northcott was sure to be laughing at someone else's expense. Someone like her, to be exact, she thought with an inner sniff, even as she was carefully maintaining a polite façade.

Perhaps not as well as she had thought, she realized as it appeared that his amusement deepened. Her chin lifted automatically. She wouldn't allow the arrogant man to laugh at her. She didn't care if everyone else at this terrible event thought her to be beneath them, but she wouldn't tolerate it in this particular member of Society.

There was just something about Gilbert Northcott that Caroline couldn't quite put her finger on that set her teeth on edge whenever she was near him. She didn't think it was how very handsome he was, although that was undoubtably a contributing factor. It seemed to her that he was play acting. If she had been asked, she wouldn't be able to provide any evidence as to why she thought it, but even though he appeared to be a veritable fop or dandy, always more concerned about his clothes, straightening his cuffs, or observing others through his quizzing glass, Caroline had the very distinct impression that it was an act intended to distract everyone from his very intelligent gaze. Most would say he didn't have an intelligent gaze, she supposed.

Before she had a chance to open her mouth and give him a well-deserved set down, Caroline heard the small orchestra begin the strains to the next dance.

"Are you promised for this one?" Mr. Northcott asked, as though he didn't know the answer to his own question, even though they were clearly in the corner into which most of the wallflowers had congregated.

Caroline's skill of being able to smile politely while swallowing all negative feelings stood her in good stead that night. She wanted to lie, but they all knew she didn't have a dance partner lined up. Really, unless Lady St. John had specifically roped someone into dancing with her, Caroline spent her evenings on the sidelines of the dance floor, hiding from the lecherous fortune hunters, the only gentlemen who had yet taken an interest in her.

So when he held his hand out to her, there was nothing short of causing a scene that Caroline could do other than slip her own much smaller one into his and watch as it was swallowed up into his grip. Even though she was taller than the average debutante, the top of her head only came to his chin. It made him an ideal dance partner for her. She really ought to be delighted to be in the handsome man's arms. She loved to dance, and he was highly skilled at it. He was the perfect size to partner her. And he didn't stink despite the heat generated in the crowded room.

But her pride wouldn't allow her to enjoy the experience. Once more she kept her sighing silent. It wouldn't do her any good to allow her displeasure or discomfort to be visible. Lady St. John would surely wash her hands of her if she were to do so. And while Caroline wouldn't mind very much, she knew how disappointed her father would be. Never mind the fact that her mother would have been even more disappointed if she had ever thought Caroline would disrespect her dearest friend in such a way.

No, it mattered very little how Caroline felt about making her debut. She needed to find a way of making it a success. Even if it was near to killing her. Perhaps if her mother had never died she wouldn't hate the Season quite so much. If her Mama were there, they would be having a lark whether Caroline was a success or not. And of course, seeing as Mama had actually been born to this world, perhaps Caroline wouldn't have felt so completely out of place in it.

It would have been awkward for Mama, though, too, considering the fact that her family had disowned her when she had married the unknown, decidedly low class, Roger Smith. They had only forgiven her upon her death. It disgusted Caroline that somehow death could redeem someone in these people's eyes. Wouldn't it have been better to embrace her back into their lives while she had been alive? It had been difficult for Caroline to be civil when she had been introduced to her relatives by her hostess Lady St. John. She was only grateful that they hadn't tried to pursue a relationship with her. It was challenging enough being polite whenever their paths crossed. And it happened more often than she would prefer. She would prefer it to never happen. But that was impossible to arrange in the rarified world of the *ton*. Despite the seemingly large numbers of gentry that had flocked to the city, there weren't in all reality that many of them and their paths were forever intersecting.

Caroline recalled herself to the matter at hand. She was about to dance with Gilbert Northcott. And she would have to smile throughout the ordeal. Not that it was really an ordeal. He was actually a pleasure to dance with if one could ignore the man himself. Despite her life as a wallflower, she had danced once before with Mr. Northcott, at her first ball. She rather thought it had been a pity dance on his part, but that mattered very little. The man was a skilled dancer.

"Are you having a pleasant evening, Miss Smith?"

Much to her dismay, his smile produced a small dent in his cheek, almost like a dimple. Could he possibly be any more handsome? It was hardly fair. Caroline knew her face was trying to twist itself into a scowl despite her best efforts to maintain a generally neutral expression.

"Very pleasant, thank you for asking." Her reply was blander than cold oatmeal and it almost made her smile, especially when a small frown started to form between her partner's eyebrows. It might be contrarian of her, but she did enjoy confusing the man as he quite confused her.

Why would he ask her to dance? She supposed he could be sufficiently interested in her fortune to overcome the deficiencies of her background. As the younger son, it wasn't likely that he had much, if any, wealth of his own. The gossip certainly didn't speak of any as they did for his brother. It was one more thing she disliked about the *ton* – how hypocritical it was to discuss a gentleman's income while considering it beyond vulgar to talk about money in any other context.

Caroline's opinion was the complete opposite. She thought it was vulgar to discuss the contents of *anyone's* bank account. But talking about business was a sound topic to her. Not that any of the highborn agreed with her. It was one more piece of evidence that she was much more her father's daughter than her mother's. And one more thing she had learned to keep to herself after taking up residence under Lady St. John's roof.

It struck her that she ought to have asked a question of her own. Caroline wasn't sure why she was so introspective that evening. She recalled herself to her senses. Not that she wanted to encourage Mr. Northcott to be courting her, but she couldn't very well be rude to the man either.

Her smile was thin, but she made an attempt anyway. "How has your evening been thus far, Mr. Northcott? It isn't terribly often that you turn up at an entertainment such as this."

"Have you been watching for me?" From the way his eyes were dancing as he asked the question, Caroline felt once more that he was making a jest of her, and she stiffened in his arms. She managed not to miss any steps, but it was a close run thing. It was only her dread of causing a scene and offending Lady St. John that kept her from walking away from the dreadful man in the middle of their dance.

Caroline couldn't have said what was revealed on her face, but the gentleman's features changed immediately.

"My apologies," he said with a slight bow even as he carried on with the dance. "I meant you no disrespect. It was merely a jest."

She offered him a small bow of her own. Caro couldn't help but admire the magnificent way neither of them missed a single step. In fact, not that she had a vast amount of experience, but she would have to say Mr. Northcott was the best dancer she'd had the pleasure of partnering. It was quite disappointing, all things considered.

Since the Northcotts were a popular, influential family, Caroline knew it was her responsibility to keep the relationship polite even if there really wasn't a relationship to speak of. And from her weeks of experience attending balls, she suspected this particular dance was going to last at least another couple minutes even though it had already felt interminable. She needed to think of some other conversational gambit.

But what? Ought she to ask about his taste in sports? Or whether or not he had seen the latest play being presented? Or if he preferred Vauxhall? Or if he would be retiring to Bath at the end of the Season? Would it be off-putting to ask if he ever took a seat in the House of Lords considering he wasn't a Lord? Caroline felt her face twitching with her desire to laugh over the quandary she found herself in.

"What has amused you about the minuet, Miss Smith?"

Caroline twitched over his question. Ought she to be truthful?

"I was trying and failing to think of something to ask you."

She was relieved to see that his smile appeared genuine as he asked her a question. "And why was that amusing?"

Caro shrugged slightly, at a loss, but met his eye with a smile. "Because I had so many ideas but none of them seemed fitting." When his eyebrow quirked up as though in question, she had to laugh a little. "Nothing inappropriate, of course, but I wasn't sure if it would be appropriate to ask if you enjoy sports or if you have had any involvement in politics," she concluded with another shrug, feeling a little helpless. A young lady ought not think about a gentleman's involvement in the more physical sports like boxing or what have you and as a younger son, it wasn't likely he would involve himself in the House. But despite the fact that she ought not be interested, she couldn't prevent her curiosity.

To her relief, though, he laughed with her. The low, deep sound did something inexplicable to her belly, as though butterflies suddenly fluttered there, but she wasn't nervous so she couldn't explain the sudden sensation, even to herself. She tried to wipe the frown from her face even as she felt it crinkling her forehead.

"To answer some of the questions you didn't ask, you might be surprised, but I do enjoy both."

When he didn't say anything else, Caro's face split in a grin. "You aren't the most talkative gentleman I've ever met, that's for certain. Would you care to elaborate?"

"Now I'm curious as to who was the most talkative," he countered with laughter dancing in his hazel eyes. Again the flutters started up in her belly, but Caroline was slightly more prepared for them this time.

"All of them were more so than you," she replied tartly.

"Are you accusing me of being a trialsome partner, Miss Smith?"

At this point Caroline accepted that this particular dance wasn't following any of the acceptable patterns she had been taught, and she threw caution to the wind.

"Since you dance so beautifully, I wouldn't say you were trialsome exactly," she admitted, surprised when he laughed a little louder this time.

"But other than my dance skills, you wouldn't be so circumspect, is that what you are saying?"

Again she lifted one shoulder in half a shrug, not answering his question with anything other than a smile.

"One could say that you aren't very talkative either," he noted.

"I have been taught it is better to keep my thoughts to myself if they aren't of the popular variety."

"Really?" His eyebrows were now nearly reaching the swatch of hair that was threatening to tumble onto his forehead. "Now you have raised my curiosity even more. Perhaps you aren't the dull country mouse I thought you to be."

Rather than taking offence, Caroline was intrigued by his statement and tilted her head as though to examine him more closely even as a giggle rose up in her throat. Perhaps in Gilbert Northcott's case, too, there was more than met the eye...

Chapter Two

"**I**f you thought me a dullard, why on earth would you ask me to dance?"

Gil wanted to slap his own face for so allowing his tongue to run away with him. The girl's question certainly had merit.

It was far outside of his usual experience. He had learned from boyhood to keep his thoughts to himself. And to never insult a lady. Of course, Miss Smith wasn't a lady. And she didn't seem to feel insulted. But still, implying she was a dull country bumpkin was beyond rudeness. And she was a gently bred female. His mother would pull his ear if she were still on this earth to do so.

To his dismay, he could feel heat climbing the back of his neck. Now he was about to blush like a schoolgirl. That hadn't happened to him since he had gone up to Eton. This evening was going from bad to worse. And how was he to answer her? He now needed every ounce of the diplomatic skills he was reputed to have. Or he could act the part of the bored Society gentleman. He wondered which would be the best choice.

"Your dowry is reputed to be quite attractive." He allowed his voice to drawl out the statement as though it mattered very little. Which was true, of course, but no one in Society would believe it.

To his surprise, even though her cheeks turned pink and she tensed in his arms, her gaze remained steady upon his, even as her eyes narrowed slightly and again her head tilted in that way she had of appearing as though she were studying a matter.

"That isn't it, though." She said it as though she were slightly confused and puzzling through the matter.

Gilbert watched in fascination as a frown started to form between her eyebrows but then, as though she had recalled herself to her senses, she ironed out the wrinkle and presented him with a very sweet, gentle smile. Not at all what he would expect given the conversation they were having. Or not having, really. He almost shook his head but didn't want to confound her further.

"Never mind, you needn't tell me," she concluded with a dismissive little noise that he ought to find rude but instead found rather endearing. The worst of it was that it actually made him feel inclined to tell her the truth. There was no way he could tell anyone really, but certainly not a young woman of the *ton*. He knew his smile held a touch of bitterness but that couldn't be helped.

"Will you attend the balloon ascension?" He asked the question for lack of anything else to discuss as she hadn't been terribly forthcoming on any of the other topics he had proposed. Perhaps a direct question would be more successful. Gilbert himself wasn't terribly interested in such matters, but he knew his new sister-in-law would have been fascinated with the entire concept, so he had determined to attend in order to be able to tell her about it. It was sure to irritate his brother and delight his sister-in-law so it was an ideal activity.

The woman in his arms was again watching him attentively, causing Gilbert to wish he could know what she was thinking. It was a daft wish. He could never know what she was truly thinking, and he shouldn't even be interested. The only reason he had approached her was because he had just started to investigate her father. He was looking for facts not feelings, he reminded himself with a bit of disgust. Just because his brother had been caught into matrimony and now was spouting all the nonsense about his lovely young wife didn't mean Gilbert was about to get all warm and gooey about anyone's inner workings.

Oh, of course, he had to be well-versed in people's motivations and even their thought processes to a certain extent, but he confined himself for the most part to the criminal element. They were far easier to understand in his estimation. Young women, on the other hand, were far too complex and led to way too much trouble if one even started down that path. Just look at Lucian.

Gilbert knew the Office considered him to be a first-rate investigative agent and he thrived under that reputation. He prided himself on his doggedness and his success rate. But he had never been in the awkward position of having a gently bred young woman being associated with his investigation. It was her father who was the primary target of the Office's interest at the moment, but so far Gil's research indicated to him that the intelligent young woman in his arms could be just as culpable as her father. So her feelings ought not to matter in the least.

Finally, Miss Smith licked her lip as though she were suddenly nervous, and she gave her head a little shake. "No, sir, I have no intention of going anywhere near such a spectacle. I think it rather ridiculous to attempt to leave the ground. I learned that lesson as a child trying to climb trees. God intended us to keep both feet on a solid surface, in my opinion."

Gilbert grinned. He didn't completely agree with her, but he did understand the sentiment.

"Tree climbing wasn't your strength, then, I take it?"

To his surprise, rather than taking offense she returned his grin. "I broke my arm multiple times trying to perfect the art and never could manage to make it to the top."

Newfound respect touched Gilbert momentarily. "You didn't give up after the first break?"

To his surprise, the girl again gave her little half shrug that he was beginning to think was an unconscious habit. "I was a rather stubborn girl," she replied in a tone that was a combination of defiance and apology, a rare combination to be sure. "Finally my father threatened to thrash me if I tried it again. That was when my tree climbing days ended."

"So then I would actually expect you to be all the more fascinated by the balloon ascension if you had been so determined to get off the ground."

She shook her head. "No, when I accepted that the tree had finally won, I agreed with my father that my feet would never leave the earth. I shan't change that decision now no matter who has invested in the technology."

Gilbert blinked over the slightly bitter tone her voice had taken on. He again wished he knew what she was thinking but once more dismissed the strange impulse to find out. One of the reasons for his investigation into her father was tied in to his investments. And one of those investments was the balloons. Was Miss Smith opposed to her father's investments? How could he pry without revealing his own interest in the matter?

"Have you ever seen the balloons up close?"

She again appeared as uncomfortable as such a controlled person could look, but she didn't avoid his question as she had previous ones.

"I have. Have you?"

"I have as well. I thought they were quite beautiful."

She blinked at him. "You did? How strange. I thought they were garish and ugly. Horses and houses and people can be beautiful. I would never have used that description for such an unnatural device."

Gilbert laughed over her wording.

"I suppose I can see what you're saying from that perspective. But I thought it was rather graceful and elegant."

"Perhaps, but only until a rogue gale were to blow up, and then it would be anything but graceful and elegant."

"That's true. In that case, it's a very excellent thing that the scientists have grown so skilled at predicting the winds and weather."

The glance she cast him was full of such skepticism that he again had to laugh but made an effort to keep it low enough not to draw any attention to them.

"Have you truly found any weather forecasts to be sufficiently accurate that you would like to stake your life upon them?"

He smiled at her question. "Well, as I said, I will be observing, not participating in the balloon ascension."

"That is wise of you, sir, but I cannot bear the thought of being an observer if something dreadful were to go wrong. Any manner of things could happen. Do you understand the mechanisms in place to make it work?"

Gilbert frowned slightly. "I think I have a rudimentary understanding."

"Well even that is sufficient to know that several elements of the event could lead to the death of at least one person."

"How do you come to be so informed on the matter?"

"I am one of those odd creatures called a female with a brain, Mr. Northcott," she replied primly, which really didn't answer his question but caused him great amusement.

"And you used that brain to gather the information how?"

Her sigh was sufficiently dramatic to convey her wish to continue to avoid the question but finally she answered him. "My father is backing this current venture."

"Ah," Gilbert said. "And did he forbid you from involvement?"

"Not in the least. But he did refuse to listen to my long list of reasons why I didn't think he ought to have anything to do with it."

"Does he usually listen to you? From your aggrieved tone, it would imply that you were surprised by his refusal."

To Gilbert's surprise, the young woman's smile was of the sunniest nature when she turned it upon him. "I had thought he always listened to me, to be honest, at least with regards to investments. This is the first time I have ever argued so strenuously against something and he still went ahead with it. And for the life of me, I cannot understand why he was so insistent."

Gilbert had his own suppositions on the matter, but he couldn't share them with her. There were some who thought the air transportation would overtake that of rail. Considering weight limitations, Gilbert couldn't see how that would ever be possible, but he was an investigator, not a scientist.

Gilbert realized he needed to remove himself from the presence of Miss Caroline Smith. It would not do for him to become fascinated with her. For many reasons, not the least of which was his investigation. He would have to talk to his masters at the Home Office to see if he could be removed from this particular matter. It was more dangerous than he wanted to consider. Dangerous to his single status and therefore to his position within the Home Office. He had never been averse to danger before. But he would far rather stand in front of a bullet than the combination of a beautiful and intelligent young woman.

~~~

He suited the thought to actions as soon as he could get a hearing the next day but didn't get the result he'd hoped for.

"You think the daughter might be involved because she told you she is averse to hot air balloons? That is rather slim evidence, Northcott." Gilbert couldn't argue with his superior on the subject. It was just a feeling he had, there was no evidence attached to it. "You know it's the railroads we're concerned about, anyway. Nothing to do with the balloon ascension."

"I understand that, my lord, but it was just the way she said it and the watchful way she looked at me."

"Made you afeared, didn't it, young man?"

Gilbert instinctively objected but tried to keep his reaction contained. "I think Caroline Smith should be watched and because she's a gently born female, I don't feel I can be the one to do it. I have no intention to wed, but a scandal could force it upon me."

"Don't be a ninnyhammer," Lord Chamberlain scoffed. "An intelligent chit is to be admired not feared, my dear boy. But still that isn't a reason to avoid a matter. You know it's Roger Smith we're concerned about after that matter with Duncan. We have the proof about Duncan's involvement. Smith is his close associate. But since Smith is now rubbing shoulders with lords and such, some are insisting we need more evidence of his involvement before we act on it. If you think the daughter is involved, too, you can look into them both."

"I am not arguing with you on this matter, my lord. I am merely suggesting that someone else would be better suited to this particular investigation."

"Well, it's far too late to extricate yourself from it now, Northcott. You know you're one of our best agents. That's one of the reasons you were given this assignment. You are to continue your research into the Smiths when you attend the house party Lady Worth is hosting next week. As you said, if the chit is so involved in her father's business, then perhaps she *is* part of the plot, too. I don't see how a lady could be involved but befriend her. All the better to get the information we need, from my point of view."

"I wasn't going to accept that invitation, my lord."

"Well, now you are."

Gil flexed his jaw in order to prevent the rejection he wanted to utter. He loved being a part of the Home Office, and he wouldn't want to jeopardize his chance at future assignments by refusing this one, but he hated going to house parties. As the second son of an earl with very little chance of inheriting anything from anyone, he wasn't considered a great matrimonial catch, not that he wanted to be one. But his position within Society was such that when he received an invitation to such an event, he was well aware of the fact that it was only to balance the hostess' numbers. It reminded him far too much of his years growing up when he was taught all the same things as his older brother, but he was all too conscious of the fact that the only way he were to inherit was if something terrible were to happen to Lucian.

It had made him feel redundant in his own home even though he had thrown himself into learning all there was to know about the earldom. In some ways, he would make a better future earl than the heir because Lucian had been far too preoccupied with his own interests to really pay attention to the family holdings. In some ways, his brother's bad attitude made things a little easier for Gilbert. Since Lucian had paid so little attention, he would need Gilbert's help when he finally did inherit. But Gilbert knew his brother wasn't nearly as lazy and lackadaisical as he would like people to believe, and Lucian would be able to quickly learn whatever he needed to take good care of Everleigh when the time came.

All the more reason why Gilbert needed his position in the Home Office. He had managed to make some sound investments of his own, so he certainly didn't rely on the paltry wage the Office offered to its officers and agents, but the assignments gave his life direction and were the only thing that made him feel a sense of accomplishment. Thus, despite the fact that he hated the thought of attending a house party, he found himself a couple days later packing his bags and setting off to the countryside. He wondered what Miss Smith would make of his attendance and whether or not he would truly be able to find out anything about Mr. Smith while in such a setting.

Gilbert had doubted that Mr. Smith would even be in attendance since he so rarely graced the ballrooms or drawing rooms that his daughter frequented, but

Lord Chamberlain assured him he had it on good authority that the man would be present. Apparently Lady St. John had high hopes of bringing one of the gentlemen up to scratch and thus the girl's father's presence was required.

Chapter Three

Caroline had managed to avoid the balloon ascension the *ton* was agog over and two days later was bowling along with Lady St. John and their maid already rather bored of the travel. Her nails were digging into her palms in an effort to quell the tide of nerves that fluttered in her midsection. A house party sounded like exactly the worst way she could imagine spending her time. She couldn't imagine what her chaperone had been thinking to accept such an invitation. A fortnight spent in the company of the same people sounded like the utmost bore, at least if they were all Society members anyhow.

If it were to be a retreat of scientists or businessmen, then Caroline would be beside herself with delight. But Lady St. John had assured her that only the very best of the *ton* would be present. For that reason, Caro was truly skeptical about her own presence there. She wondered what her chaperone had been obliged to promise the party's host in exchange for the invitation.

Caroline admonished herself. She was being the least charitable creature on God's earth. Lady St. John, despite the fact that she wasn't the warmest woman Caro had ever spent time with, was obviously doing her best to make her charge's Season a success. Caroline ought to be grateful. And even though Caro was a wallflower and didn't feel a true part of Society, most people had actually been kind and gracious, at least to her face. Caroline was well aware that she was predisposed to dislike noble society due to her mother's family. It wasn't right to paint everyone with the same brush. And she truly shouldn't suspect that her invitation to the house party had anything to do with coercion.

Fighting the grimace that wanted to distort her face, Caroline admonished herself once more that she ought not be such a cynic. Perhaps Lady St. John was merely particular friends of the Worths. But Caroline couldn't help but suspect that somehow her father's wealth had been brought into play in connection with the invitations. And that made her want to squirm in her seat with the intense discomfort that only an outsider could feel. It was odd, really. It seemed her father's money was acceptable when it was of benefit to someone, but the bourgeois source of it put her just slightly outside of fully acceptable.

But there had been no argument she could think of that prevented her from sitting across from her chaperones on the backward facing seat in the blessedly well sprung carriage as they made their way inexorably west toward the Worths' seemingly sprawling country estate. Lady St. John hadn't been fully informed of everyone who had been invited but the names she had mentioned had led Caroline to believe it would either be a very large house or a very crowded house. Or perhaps both, she surmised with another suppressed grimace. And then she would have lost two entire weeks of opportunities to find a husband she could accept if no one present actually ended up being acceptable to or interested in her.

"You needn't look so very despondent about this, my dear. I am certain you shall enjoy this visit." Despite Caroline's connections to the bourgeois, Lady St. John's long-ago friendship with Caroline's mother made her try to be kind to the young woman. But Caro was uncomfortably aware that it was an effort for the elegant viscountess. And while Caroline would almost rather wait another year before choosing a husband, she was beginning to suspect that her hostess was determined to fire her off that Season in order to leave the way open for her own daughter's debut.

It wasn't that Caroline would object in any way to Esther's company. She quite liked the younger girl and thought it would be far more enjoyable to attend events such as these with another girl. But the fact that Esther had been made to stay at home rather than accompany her mother and their guest to London for the Season made Caroline suspect Lady St. John didn't want Esther's name associated with her own. It was the most lowering thought and did nothing to bolster her confidence as they neared their destination. She really ought to ask her straight out, but Caro wasn't sure her feelings could endure the confirmation.

"Caroline, do tell me why you appear as though we are approaching the guillotine rather than a lovely break from the social whirl. I thought you didn't enjoy all the events we've been attending. I actually thought you would welcome this respite."

Caroline felt swamped with guilt, and she reached across the carriage to clasp her hostess' hand.

"My dear lady, I do apologize for my lack of gratitude. In fact, I am exceedingly grateful for all that you have done for me. I just fear that I'm missing the opportunity to meet the right man by taking a break from it all."

"Perhaps you will meet him here. Or you've already met him and will become better acquainted during this visit and will decide that you will suit quite well. Did you not think this might be a better experience? A ball is hardly the best environment for getting to know someone beyond their dance skills."

Caroline let go of Lady St. John's hand and sat back into her corner but still held her gaze and smiled at her with as much affection as she could muster. Despite the older woman's aversion to her guest's background, Caro knew she was trying her best for her deceased friend's daughter. Caroline couldn't blame the woman for her feelings. Everyone else in the *ton* seemed to feel the same way. She couldn't imagine how either Lady St. John or her father thought they would be able to marry her off respectably considering everyone thought her barely respectable.

And Caroline didn't want to be married just for her father's money. There were gentlemen who had been paying her court when she first appeared in Society, who were barely accepted socially but who had thought her father's money would make an excellent addition to their estates. Caroline was relieved that both Lady St. John and her father had deemed them unacceptable. At least her father wasn't that desperate for a title in the family.

She rather thought she had much to offer any man as his wife. Even though most thought being well-educated wasn't a desirable quality, Caroline couldn't agree. She was well read, articulate, and well versed in all that was required to run a large household. Besides that, she knew how to balance a ledger and had enough knowledge of all her father's investments to be able to make sound business decisions. Caroline had a hard time not resenting the fact that most men didn't consider that an asset. It made her wonder what her father and Lady St. John were thinking to try to wed her to any of these men. But surely she would be able to find one she could consider tolerable.

"You are quite right, my lady, and I do apologize for my lack of enthusiasm. I am merely intimidated by the company I shall be keeping. But I know you are doing your best to provide for my future, and I do appreciate that. I trust you will see your way clear to advise me once we arrive and see who else is present."

"Of course, my dear. It is what your mother would have wanted." The smile the viscountess offered Caroline was tremulous at best. Every time she mentioned her old friend, tears sprang to her eyes instantly. It made Caro wonder just what the nature of their friendship had been. Either the older woman was loyal to a fault or she was labouring under a heavy burden of guilt for some past slight. Caroline was inclined to believe that Lady St. John had probably cut off contact with her mother when she had dared to wed the very non-nobility Roger Smith, just like everyone else in her life. Obviously they had later resumed contact as Caroline had the old letters to prove it. And the noblewoman had taken an interest in Caroline from her childhood on, remaining in touch with her father after her mother's death in order to keep track of Caroline. For that, Caro had to love the woman, even if she didn't share most of her views.

"Did you and my mother ever attend a house party together?"

Caroline always hesitated to ask the other woman questions like that for fear of the tears it might produce, but since Lady St. John had already brought her up, she figured it wouldn't cause any further harm.

With relief Caro saw that the viscountess had her tears under control as she smiled in recollection. "We did. It was quite the best time we had, I dare say. Which is part of why I was so determined for you to have this experience. I know you will enjoy it just as we did."

Caroline didn't bother to reply to that. Lady St. John had never been able to accept that Caro was really nothing like her dear mother. She was far too much her father's daughter. "Do you have any idea of the sorts of activities we can expect?"

"I am sure there will be riding and dances and shuttlecock. Perhaps drawing or music. Quiet conversation and boisterous laughter. It is the very nature of a house party that means it all depends on who your fellow guests are."

"I do hope ours will be of the very best nature."

"I am sure they will be. Our hostess has assured me we shall be well pleased."

"It is rather odd that she didn't have a complete list to share with you, though, isn't it?" The unknown was part of the reason for Caroline's trepidation. She would far rather know for certain who they would be obliged to spend the next fortnight with.

"Not everyone had replied when we spoke," Lady St. John answered, turning her eyes back to the scenery passing by her window. Caroline narrowed her eyes at the older woman's profile. Her suspicions were growing that there was something her chaperone didn't want to share with her. Her stomach was going to cramp if she didn't alleviate the nerves fluttering there.

"Have you been to their estate before?" Caroline finally asked.

"Not in years, but I haven't heard of any extensive renovations so it is likely to be unchanged."

"Can you tell me what it's like?"

Caroline tried to quell her nerves, but she clearly hadn't been successful when Lady St. John smiled at her. "My dear girl, you really need to get over whatever is causing you to be so anxious. Our destination is a beautiful, large estate, but that will be nothing new for you. You have lived in far larger and more complicated homes since you were a child. You will not get lost, you will not do anything socially unacceptable, and you will be charming at all times. This I know."

"Thank you, my lady," Caroline murmured as she tried to convince her clenched fingers to loosen.

"Tell me what is bothering you so, child."

Now it was Caroline's turn to have tears well in her eyes. It was so rare that anyone was soft or gentle with her. Most were cool, and her father was always tough no matter the circumstances. Since her mother's death, Caro had grown accustomed to there being nothing gentle in her life. But that didn't mean she enjoyed it. All her defenses crumbled at the viscountess' gentle command. Taking a deep breath, it felt as though she were making a confession.

"I truly hate being tolerated, my lady. I want to be welcomed and appreciated, if not loved. I'm afraid I will feel like an outcast for the entire fortnight. And there will be no respite. At least if I have to endure that sensation at a ball or a breakfast or some such, I can always leave and have a break from it all. A house party means there is no escape."

"Oh, my poor dear, do you truly feel that way amongst Society?"

Caroline couldn't meet the other woman's gaze. She didn't want to tell Lady St. John that she herself made her feel that way. So she just nodded and allowed the woman to take that how she would.

"Well, I love you, Caroline, and I'm certain the others will, too."

Blinking back the moisture from her eyes, Caroline didn't snort her disbelief, but it was a close run thing.

"Thank you, my lady," she managed to say again, not offering the arguments that sprang to her tongue.

"I'm sorry I don't have the full guest list to share with you, if that would somehow make you more comfortable. I should have thought to write and ask for it after we accepted the invitation."

Caroline shrugged. "It probably wouldn't make a great deal of difference. I would be nervous either way." She concluded with a small laugh.

"Does knowing your father will be there make you more or less nervous?" Lady St. John was curious.

Caroline offered a shrug even though she knew it wasn't the viscountess' favorite gesture. "A bit of both. I love my father a great deal, but I know he isn't a Society favorite. So I'm afraid it will be extra awkward with him present. But it is for the best. He is my father. Any potential suitors would have to accept that."

"Yes, that was my thought as well. And I am hopeful there might be some actual contenders for your hand. Having your father there will make any declarations far easier."

Her smile felt forced, but Caroline offered it anyway. She couldn't help but wish her father didn't so desperately want for her to wed a gentleman. But she had worn herself out arguing the topic to no avail. And she had long ago accepted that she must wed. She didn't relish being even more strange than everyone already considered her. Marriage was a must for a gently bred female. Even one in as precarious a position as she.

For the briefest moment her mind flitted to Gilbert Northcott. She couldn't have even explained why. But after their dance the week prior, he was often preying upon her mind. The dance hadn't even been that memorable aside from his excelling skill. They hadn't discussed anything of import, and she was reasonably sure he had lied to her. But still she thought of him. Perhaps *because* of the lie. Why would he do so? Why was mention of her large dowry a lie? She knew it was the main reason any gentleman showed any interest in her, so it didn't even bother her overly anymore. So why did Mr. Northcott use that as an excuse?

Pondering the matter over and over hadn't helped her reach any conclusions. Caroline was hoping the fortnight away from Town would help her overcome the tendency to dwell upon the handsome man. He was certainly not one of the candidates for her hand, she was sure of that even though she was pretty sure her father would be delighted at the prospect, despite the man's lack of title. Mr. Rogers would probably consider his proximity to an earl and a viscount to be good enough.

Not that there was an overabundance of suitable men striving to claim her hand in marriage. There were a few truly unacceptable fortune hunters who had bothered her during the first two weeks of her debut, but Lady St. John had dealt with them quite handily. Caroline wasn't even sure how she had done so. She ought to ask her. Perhaps she would when the dust of her Season had settled. Right now everything felt much too raw, and she didn't think she would be able to ask without revealing her pent up emotions to her hostess.

"Why has it been so long since you've been to Chester Hill?" she finally thought to ask, hoping to maintain the open lines of communication with the older woman.

Lady St. John shrugged, much to Caroline's surprise. She thought the very proper woman considered such a gesture to be unacceptable. Surprising her further, the viscountess grinned.

"Our hostess considers herself to be a matchmaker. She doesn't proclaim her intentions, but every year there is at least one betrothal after her house party. Since I was married, until now, I haven't been in the position of searching for a match."

Caroline laughed lightly. "So you might be in attendance for a few years in a row, if that's the case."

Lady St. John's smile dimmed slightly. "I am unsure if Esther will be ready for a house party next year."

Caroline kept her smile in place with effort. The darling daughter of the house would clearly not be forced into anything, unlike the unwelcome imposter, she thought bitterly. Something of her feelings must have displayed themselves upon her face because Lady St. John was quick to add to her statement.

"Surely you realize the girl is far more timid than you could ever be. I quite despair of her to be honest."

"Perhaps we should have brought her with us. She could get a taste for Society life," Caro answered lightly, even though she knew the older woman didn't really want her daughter to be tainted by the association. Or perhaps, once again Caroline was allowing her prejudice to show. She shouldn't have such harsh feelings toward her generous hostess. She turned her gaze to the opposite window to ponder her thoughts. It must be a challenge to be so torn in one's intentions, she realized of her hostess. The poor woman was determined to do what she considered her duty for her late friend's daughter. But she didn't approve of her guest. What a quandary. Caroline's empathy for her hostess grew, and she was more determined than ever to find her match as quickly as possible.

If only a gentleman they could all agree upon would present himself.

Chapter Four

G ilbert was windblown and dusty but in a much better frame of mind by the time he arrived at Chester Hill. He was impressed that his hostess had barely wrinkled her nose at the sight of him. But he also appreciated the speed in which he had been whisked off to his room in order to become more presentable. His valet hadn't yet arrived, but a servant was assigned to assist him in the meantime. Used to doing for himself despite the household he had grown up in, Gil was soon tidied and ready for company, but he lingered in his room after dismissing the servant. Even though he had accepted this assignment with as much good grace as he could muster, he was reluctant to get started.

How was he to investigate Roger Smith at a crowded house party? That was the question he had repeatedly flung at his superiors over the days between being given the assignment and his departure for Chester Hill. He had been assured again and again that he merely had to watch and see who the other man interacted with. Apparently Gilbert was the only agent available who would be able to gain an invitation to the exclusive event. So it wasn't his skill or his reputation as an investigator that had gained him the assignment. Once more, he was nearly redundant. His stomach cramped at the unwelcome thought, and he pushed it away as best he could.

Redundant or not, he had accepted the assignment and needed to do his best to see it through.

He gave his head a shake. He was being ridiculous. It was just an assignment, the same as any other he had been given, Gilbert assured himself. There was no need for him to become missish on the matter. With one more glance down his person to ensure he would pass anyone's exacting judgment, Gil left his room to find out whether or not his quarry had yet arrived.

Chester Hill was a spectacular estate. Everything except the wall hangings was made of sandstone that had probably been dug from the surrounding hillside. It was a rich colour, warmer than some he'd seen. It leant an attractive glow to the large house, making it far more appealing than such a large edifice would often carry. Even though he was sure there must be at least twenty or thirty guest rooms besides the family wing, it still felt almost quaint.

Gilbert wondered if that impression would turn out to be deceiving or if it was an accurate assessment. Since it was the current residents' ancestors who had arranged for the house, it was entirely possible that the previous occupants were far more appealing than his host and hostess. Not that he meant to imply, even within his own thoughts that the Worths were unattractive or unwelcoming. While Lady Worth had been a bit taken aback by his turning up in her salon with travel dust still clinging to him, she hadn't banished him for the *faux pas*.

He had two weeks to decide what he thought of his hostess and host, he reminded himself even as he drew all sorts of conclusions as he walked through their house. For one thing, he could hear a few footmen and maids whistling or humming. That struck him as evidence that the servants were comfortable in their work even when the household was expecting a large influx of guests. That would suggest that Lady Worth wasn't so very exacting as he might have thought.

Perhaps she wouldn't take offense if she were to find out that he was conducting an investigation under her roof in the guise of being a guest at her party. Of course, considering he hadn't necessarily been on her original guest list, she must have some sort of thoughts about how he came to be one of her guests. Gilbert doubted Lord Worth was in the habit of adding to her numbers. Or perhaps he was. Gilbert was a worker bee, not a member of the oversight in the Home Office. Unlike his brother. Not that Lucian was really in oversight, but his title and position brought with it more authority even in the milieu where one's qualifications and abilities should carry more weight than the circumstances of one's birth.

Gilbert tried not to be bitter but it was a challenge some days.

Today was one of those days.

He could never quite turn off the investigator side of his brain. It had always been that way for him, even before becoming an agent. It was all the worse now. He found himself wondering about the other guests, not just the Smiths. While he had seen the evidence against Duncan's involvement in the plot against the rail system and was aware of Duncan and Smith's previous business associations, Gilbert didn't think that was enough to go on. He agreed more evidence was needed before an accusation could be made. He also thought there was a possibility they were off on their suppositions. He would take this fortnight and consider everyone present a potential suspect.

He had more questions than answers, and he didn't enjoy that sensation when he was entering into what could be a dangerous situation involving many innocent people, not the least of whom was his hostess, and it felt to him that he didn't have enough information.

He ought to have demanded that he at least be provided a full background on all who would be expected to attend. Instead, he had been given the expected guest list. But he hadn't been on that list, so he knew it wasn't complete. Besides that, a property this size would have dozens, possibly even a hundred or more servants. One or two extra people might not be noticed by anyone because large houses such as this often hired extra staff for such occasions as extra guests. Then too, the extra guests would have brought their own servants with them.

Gilbert never liked to be investigating anyone who could be considered a member of Society. And yet here he was about to carry out a mission during a *tonnish* house party, investigating the father of one of the Season's debutantes. If he gave the matter too much thought, he was sure to develop hives. There were at least a dozen things that could go wrong, not the least of which could be the ruination of a gently bred young woman if they were completely off track about the Smiths involvement in the plot against the railroads.

Or he could find himself leg-shackled.

He had tried to issue that objection with his superiors, but all they had been able to say was that it seemed to suit his brother and who was he to object if Viscount Adelaide hadn't. That argument hadn't sat well with him, but he had managed to swallow his spleen and not get himself charged with insurrection.

Clearing his thoughts and pinning a practiced, pleasant smile to his face, Gilbert retraced his steps to the salon where Lady Worth was still awaiting her arriving guests. A part of him felt badly for the poor woman. It must be a deadly dull way to spend the day as there was no way of knowing exactly when the guests would arrive.

"Welcome, again, Mr. Northcott," Lady Worth greeted him upon his return. "Could I offer you some tea or something more extensive if you haven't yet been fed?"

"Thank you for your warm hospitality, my lady," he answered without really answering as he bowed over her hand. "I appreciate your having me."

"Of course," she answered. "I was acquainted with your dear mother. Any one of her boys is always welcome in this house."

This surprised him and brought a lump to Gilbert's throat that he had to swallow down with a little difficulty.

"A cup of tea would be welcome, thank you," he managed to say. His hostess had seemed to be surprised by her own words and appeared happy to have something to do with her hands all of a sudden.

"Was your ride uneventful?" Lady Worth queried as she passed the delicate cup over into his large hands.

"It was very pleasant," Gilbert answered with a grin. "I haven't been out in this direction in quite some time, so I very much enjoyed the ride."

"It is a bit far for riding all the way, though, isn't it?"

Gilbert lifted one shoulder. "Not terribly," he answered with a smile.

Lady Worth shuddered delicately. "I cannot even imagine. I would have to take to my bed for a week if I were to even attempt such a feat."

"Come now, my lady, I don't believe that for a moment. If you have the mettle to plan and host such a large gathering as a full house party, a ride down from London should be nothing in comparison."

The older woman chuckled. "I guess it goes to show that we each have our strengths. I do hope your horse will be ready for another ride in a day or two."

"Oh yes, I didn't push him overly, despite the distance. He'll be ready to go even by tomorrow. It looked to me like your stable hands were well able to get him back in shape."

Gilbert had been in Society for several years and was quite comfortable with lavishing compliments upon a preening hostess. Complimenting a woman's staff was one sure way to get into her good graces.

Lady Worth wasn't a simpleton, though, and she cast him a shrewd glance even as she accepted his words. "Are you able to promise me you shan't be stirring up trouble while you're under my roof, Mr. Northcott?"

His eyebrows rose despite his best efforts to hide his reaction. "I am the least troublesome guest you could possibly imagine," he protested.

Lady Worth giggled girlishly. "I strongly doubt that, but I shall reserve my judgment for now."

Gilbert was relieved to hear the clatter of more arriving guests, and he moved into the room to greet others already there. The room was so expansive he hadn't even realized there were so many milling about. He nodded to various acquaintances as he scanned the current occupants of the room hiding his surprise at who he found present. Clearly the list he had been given had not been updated.

It wasn't a surprise to find that he knew or was at least acquainted with everyone there. It was a rarified world in the *ton* and it would have been a stretch of the imagination to think that Lady Worth would have invited anyone to her party who wasn't a member. He had thought perhaps there could be young women included who hadn't yet made their debut. And it was possible that some of the surrounding gentry might be included in the coming days. Those would be people he might not have met before, but it didn't appear as though any of them were present as of yet.

With his position at the Home Office, he had become very practiced at remembering faces and names, but it had also been borne upon him from childhood that it was exceedingly rude to forget someone's name. Gilbert suspected his mother must have had an uncomfortable or embarrassing encounter as a young lady, since it seemed so very important to her that none of her sons would ever tell a young woman he didn't remember her name. Gil had taken that training an extra step further and ensured he would never find himself in that awkward situation with anyone, male or female.

He knew his mother had been most concerned about young women's fragile sensitivities, but to Gilbert's way of thinking, no one wanted to think they were forgettable.

Gilbert could only hope his face remained neutral as he was surprised to note some of his fellow guests. Lady Fanny was there. That was sure to stir up all sorts of trouble. The young woman at her side looked terribly uncomfortable. He had thought there was no one he hadn't yet met, but he was reasonably sure the girl wasn't one he'd been previously introduced to. Which meant she had not yet actually made her debut. Were they hoping to get her married off without even having a Season? He wondered what the circumstances might be behind such a manoeuvre. It could just be that the girl needed a little polish before going up to Town and her aunt thought to get that for her in the more exclusive environment of the well-born house party. It would be interesting to watch the girl for the fortnight, whichever scenario was the truth. It was entirely possible that the true state of affairs was somewhere in the middle. As Gilbert was well aware, things were almost never truly black or white, always shades of grey.

To his surprise, there were other attendees he had never yet met. A handsome young pair standing by the unlit fireplace were very obviously siblings from their striking resemblance to one another. He had been informed that two of the Worth's grandchildren would be present for the festivities. From the shape of the young people's nose and chin, Gilbert rather thought these would be the youngsters in question. Perhaps not as young as first glance might have implied, he realized after further examination, and wondered absently why he had never met them. It would be more than unusual for the grandchildren of a Marquis not to go into Society even if they weren't in line to inherit. The young woman, especially, should have been brought out by now, he thought, trying to keep a frown from his features. There were turning out to be many curiosities at this particular gathering. Suddenly he remembered that the younger pair's mother had died a year ago. Perhaps she had also been ill for a time; he wasn't sure of the details. But that would explain their absence from Society. Their grandmother was probably using this occasion as a means of starting the process.

Aside from Almack's or a few very large balls, Gil had never been in attendance with such a high percentage of inexperienced Society members. It was sure to be a fascinating few days, he thought with a smile as he continued his perusal of the other guests.

Baron Crothers, he saw was taking tea with Mrs. Nesbitt and her daughter Miss Samantha Nesbitt, a pleasant young woman in her first Season. The baron was in his mid-twenties and had inherited his father's estate six years prior. From what Gilbert had heard, the young gentleman had taken to his responsibilities quite well and his estate, quite extensive for a barony, was thriving under his management. Gil supposed the man had decided it was time to take the next step in securing his succession. Gilbert was relieved to note that as the younger son, this wasn't a concern he needed to give any thought to. Since his brother had recently wed, surely the need for heirs would soon be taken care of.

He had met the Nesbitt women at previous events and had even danced with Miss Nesbitt, although he tried to keep himself quite distanced from debutantes as he had no desire to instill false hopes in anyone. Gilbert had no intention or desire to ever marry. He knew some agents juggled a family along with their responsibilities to the Crown. He didn't intend to be one of them. That was part of why he had been so determined not to attend this house party. Yet here he was. He studiously avoided making eye contact with either Nesbitt woman. They were pretty and pleasant and looking for a suitable mate. He was not it.

"Surprising to find you here, Northcott."

Gilbert turned around even as he felt a smile tugging at his mouth.

"Thornwood," he exclaimed. "I'm nearly as surprised to find you here."

Viscount Thornwood was notorious for avoiding the Marriage Mart. Gilbert stifled laughter as he watched pink shade his friend's cheeks. The other man fidgeted slightly and reached up to brush an unruly lock of his brown hair that was always tumbling upon his forehead. It was a familiar gesture that Gil had been watching since they were boys at school together.

Not wishing to tease the quieter man, Gil slapped him on the shoulder. He supposed the viscount was in the same shoes as Baron Crothers – time to start filling their nurseries. Gil was again reminded of their differences but ignored the suddenly lonely sensation that threatened him, smiling at his friend instead.

"I'm pleased to see a friend here, Thorn. I had thought to be the only one of our group in these parts."

"What group, Northcott? You were always a man apart, and well you know it. Even as a boy you had such a wall around yourself. But I can't argue with you about being pleased. I think your being here will make this a far more enjoyable sojourn in the countryside."

"I haven't seen you in an age. You weren't in Town for the sitting of the Lords?"

"Not this year. Had to send a steward," the young nobleman admitted. "I hate doing that, but there's only so many places a man can be."

"Troubles on the estate?"

The viscount bobbed his head in acknowledgement but didn't elaborate. "Mostly under control now, so I took the opportunity to take a break when I received Lady Worth's invitation."

"Hoping to gain a helpmeet, are you, Thorn?"

Again pink tinged his friend's cheekbones, but he didn't look ashamed despite his slight embarrassment.

"It's the way of things, Northcott, and well you know it."

Gilbert again felt a touch of loneliness that he quickly quelled with another forced smile. "Well, I'll wish you good hunting, then, my lord."

Lord Thornwood grinned at his friend and nodded his head, accepting his fate with good grace. With his friend in mind, Gilbert looked back at the assembled guests, wondering which might be a good match for the viscount. He hoped the other man could find a lady who wouldn't be more trouble than she was worth. Lord and Lady Mathers caught his eye. Their daughter, Lady Isabella, had made her debut that year and hadn't struck him as being completely ridiculous. Not that Gilbert would have any spare time or headspace that fortnight, but perhaps he could play matchmaker for his friend if the opportunity arose. Either way, he was reassured that there would be moments of diversion in between his forays into investigating the Smiths.

Who had not yet arrived, he was reminded as he again scanned the gathered nobles. His eyes narrowed back onto his friend. Thorn had the intelligence required for a plot. But Gil had a hard time considering the viscount capable of such underhanded dealings. He gave his head a shake.

Gilbert couldn't help worrying that he had been given bad information. What if the Smiths weren't actually attending this house party? He would be stuck there for two weeks cooling his heels for no reason other than he had obeyed an order from his superiors.

His gut began to churn at the dreadful possibility. Should he have asked more questions? Demanded more answers? Of course he should have, but he was so dependent upon his position at the Home Office. He really ought to extricate his personal sense of well-being from the assignments he received. One day he might become too old to perform such duties and then where would he be?

But for now, he would do everything he could to fulfill the duties that gave him such a great sense of purpose. Far more than when he was doing his brother's work for him upon their father's estate.

Gilbert shut down the unproductive thoughts. They were even less productive than worrying the Smiths might not turn up. He trusted the other officers at the Home Office. He hadn't been given bad information, he was certain of that. And, in either case, this wouldn't be a life and death matter, not like when his brother hadn't been informed that an enemy had escaped observation and had turned up in London to confront him. That had been a true problem. This was not.

If worse came to worst, Gil would think of some excuse to leave. Or he would stay and consider it a break from the mundane. His overseers couldn't blame him if they thought it was a waste of his time. He knew Lord Worth wouldn't thank him for upsetting his wife's numbers.

Just as he was churning all these thoughts through his mind and trying to reassure himself that he wouldn't be behind in his investigation whatever was to happen, Gilbert heard the clatter of more arriving guests. Lady Worth regained her feet and turned to the door to welcome them.

Gilbert sucked in his breath as he realized it was just who he had been awaiting, but he hadn't expected to find the chit so very attractive even though that very concern had been one of his reasons for being tempted to decline this assignment.

Not that he had been waiting for Miss Smith, he reminded himself. It was her father he was so keenly interested in. And he was looking forward to the sojourn in the country to get to know the man and ascertain whether or not he was the threat the Office thought he might be. Despite his suspicion that Miss Caroline Smith was more involved in her father's affairs than anyone let on, it was Roger Smith who was under suspicion for potential sabotage.

Chapter Five

C aroline was tired and felt more rumpled than she could tolerate. The drive to Chester Hill had been more arduous than she had anticipated. But it had had its good moments, too. She had deeply appreciated Lady St. John's attempts to be kind. And the older woman's effort to help her see the house party in a different light had paid off. But for that reason, she was less than pleased to see that their hostess was receiving them in the salon where the other guests were already assembled.

A glance down her person assured Caroline that she was as rumpled as she felt. She was used to the finest fabrics and the best servants to care for them. She wasn't used to sitting in tight quarters for upwards of eight hours and then needing to be sociable.

Her smile felt tight, but she did her best to keep it in place as her eyes flitted about the room as they approached their hostess.

She spied Gilbert Northcott almost immediately. Caro had not anticipated that possibility in the least. Her heart fluttered in her chest bringing a fleeting frown to her face. It couldn't possibly be healthy to have one's heart do unnatural acrobatics. She tore her gaze away from his and hoped he hadn't noticed. It was likely a futile hope as the man seemed to be always so watchful. It was a quality she appreciated as she liked to consider herself such as well. But if it was her he was watching, she was far less impressed. There was nothing about her that needed keen observation.

It took effort, but she ensured her eyes did not stray toward that particular gentleman once more as she curtsied before Lady Worth.

"Thank you for the invitation, my lady," she murmured, pleased to hear the note of sincerity she had been able to infuse. Further pleased to see the marchioness' answering smile appeared genuine as well. Caroline hated to think their place on the guest list had been paid for by her father's riches and influence and hoped there was at least an element of welcome for her own self somewhere in the mix.

Shrugging off the unusually melancholy thoughts, Caroline exerted herself to engage with their hostess.

"I am happy to be in the country for a time. This is the longest I've spent in Town at once, and it is pleasant to look forward to many days of quiet and fresh air."

Lady Worth laughed. "I cannot guarantee it will be terribly quiet here, though, Miss Smith. I do hope you shan't be too disappointed if the plans we have made keep you busier than you'd expected."

"Oh, no, my lady, it wasn't that sort of quiet I was speaking of. I shall look forward to whatever you have planned," she assured the hostess, silently kicking herself for having said the wrong thing.

The marchioness nodded her approval, relieving Caroline of some of her worries before the older woman's gaze turned searching.

"You don't look much the worse for wear from your travels, but would you like to be shown to your rooms in order to rest or change or anything?"

Caroline had stepped back in order to allow Lady St. John to greet her old friend and left the question to that lady to answer. For the most part, Caroline would like to take to her bed after the long, boring drive. She would also love to have a full bath. But it was doubtful she would be allowed to do either of those. Instead, she would settle for a wash basin and a comb if Lady St. John agreed to have them shown to their room. Caro held her breath awaiting the answer.

"Thank you, my dear, that would be lovely," came the viscountess' soft reply to their hostess' offer.

Before leaving the room, Caroline managed to curtsy to the assembled guests without looking at any one person in any detail, thus managing to continue to keep her gaze from encountering that of Mr. Northcott. She couldn't have even said why she was so determined to avoid him, she just knew she felt an instinctive fear of the man. But it wasn't a scared sort of fear. It was a puzzlement, in all honesty. And Caroline didn't love puzzles. She much preferred things to be straightforward and matter of fact. It was a big part of why she didn't agree fully with her father's determination for her to marry into the nobility. She would forever be obliged to tolerate such roundaboutations. It was not the happiest prospect for her to contemplate.

"You did well, child," Lady St. John complimented her as they followed the footman through the maze of the large house.

Caroline nearly missed a step as she hurried along in the viscountess' wake, so surprised was she by the older woman's words. It wasn't that Lady St. John was so very stingy with her compliments, but Caroline had truly been under the impression that her chaperone didn't really approve of her. It was reassuring to know she could see some good in her charge despite her dubious parentage.

It had been a relief to hear nothing from her father as they had greeted their hostess. Caroline hated feeling that way. She adored her father but had come to realize that the *ton* did not approve of him in the least. And he couldn't seem to accept that they didn't appreciate his speeches.

Mr. Smith loved to expound. He would have made an excellent barrister. Or a politician, Caroline thought with a smile. Anything that would have allowed him to argue for a living.

She supposed, though, that he did argue for a living, considering how many deals he negotiated in a given week or month. Caroline actually loved watching and listening to him work out his business and hated that she wasn't allowed to participate. She should have been her father's son. Then she would never have to make her debut and try to marry into a Society that couldn't really accept her.

It was her father's one weakness. He hoped to gain acceptance through his daughter. But Caroline doubted it would ever happen. Oh, she knew she would probably wed. Her dowry was attractive enough that there would eventually be someone they could agree upon. But that didn't mean Roger Smith would ever be truly welcomed into the drawing rooms of the *ton*. And even if he ever were, it wouldn't change what had happened to her mother when she had chosen to wed with the lowborn businessman.

This was exactly why she didn't ever wish to marry for love, why any man who caused any sort of flutter within her was off limits. Caro's mother had loved Roger Smith quite desperately. And they had all paid a very high price for that love.

Caroline's father had been able to overcome the efforts to put him out of business. In fact, it seemed as though the wily man had thrived on the challenge. Caro was certain his bank accounts were fuller today than they would have been if there had never been such opposition. But Caroline and her mother had paid a heavier price.

Lady Felicity, Caroline's mother, was from a very old aristocratic family. Her father, the Earl of Calwell, had not taken well to his daughter wanting to wed a commoner. When they had run away together, the old earl had done everything in his power to make her come home and disavow her husband. When that hadn't worked, he had tried to ruin Mr. Smith financially. Caroline suspected the family might have forgiven all if they had been able to feel that they had "rescued" their daughter. Instead, Felicity had happily settled in to her new life with her husband and soon their daughter. But eventually she began to miss her family. The young mother couldn't understand why her family didn't want to meet her daughter. She had also been determined to have more children. Caroline suspected that it was the loss of her other family that made her so desperate for a large family of her own. It was that desperation that had finally killed her.

One more reason why Caroline would never love a man.

If only her father would allow her to wed one of his business associates. To her, it seemed the perfect solution. She could find one who would respect her for the knowledge she had of her father's enterprises rather than judge her as less than for that very knowledge. She would feel as though she were bringing great value to the partnership. Instead, she would likely feel an outcast for the rest of her life.

Giving her head a shake, Caroline tried to rid herself of the unhelpful thoughts as her maid helped her shed the travel dirt from her person. Washing her face and hands with the cool water and soft cloth did much to restore her equilibrium. She needed to stop lamenting. She had accepted her father's decree that she not wed a businessman like himself. She needed to focus on the positive. At least he hadn't determined that she find a love match.

Caroline knew she was an intelligent young woman. Surely she could find a gentleman who would respect that. It couldn't possibly be unheard of for a nobleman to view his wife as a partner in his life rather than a vessel for his heirs and a means of refilling his coffers.

Her smile in the reflection was bitter, and Caroline did her best to right it.

"Thank you, Millie. I am delighted with your help as always."

"I didn't do much, Miss, but thank you for saying so." She jabbed one more pin into the back of Caro's coiffeur before continuing. "I don't know how you're going to carry on this evening, Miss. I'm ready for my bed after the drive, and I don't have to even leave this room if I don't want."

"But unfortunately you can't take to your bed until I do, as I doubt I'll be able to get myself out of this gown without assistance."

Millie laughed. "Of course not, but I don't have to be sociable like you do when all I want to do is growl at everyone."

Caroline smiled. "Hopefully there won't be any growling except perhaps my stomach. I doubt it will be a late night tonight as everyone is likely to be in a similar circumstance of having travelled at least some distance today. And surely Lady Worth won't have too much planned for the morning tomorrow so we should be able to recover nicely."

"Just don't forget you can plead a headache and no one will think less of you," Millie reminded her.

"My father would," Caroline countered. "But I thank you for your concern. I'm sure it'll be fine."

Caroline did appreciate the servant's concern and cherished the sensation of care for a moment before she gained her feet. She needed to return below to the gathered guests. She hadn't been brought here to spend time in her room.

Straightening her shoulders and lifting her chin, Caroline felt a little as though she were about to go into battle. It might be a daft sensation, but she couldn't get the analogy from her mind. The maid sensed her disquiet and offered her a reassuring smile.

"You look perfect, Miss, and everyone is going to love you."

Caroline's smile was weak, but she offered it anyway. She wasn't sure how she felt about the servant's words. It was kind of her to try to be friendly, but Caro wasn't sure she wanted the noble guests' love. Their respect would please her immensely, but she wasn't certain it was on offer. But that wasn't Millie's fault or problem.

"Feel free to have a lie down once you've finished with your duties."

The servant looked slightly horrified at the suggestion but then grinned and bobbed a curtsey to her mistress.

The viscountess was waiting for her.

"I'm sorry if I kept you waiting, my lady."

"Not at all, child. I could have knocked if I'd wanted you to hurry," she said with a pleasant smile before adding, "I was admiring the artwork. I had forgotten what a lovely and extensive collection they have here. And if I'm not mistaken, it has been added to or at least rearranged since I was here last."

As she spoke, Lady St. John gestured along the hallway. Caroline hadn't noticed when they had been escorted to their rooms, but she could see why the older woman was so absorbed. Many of the pieces were truly spectacular. And it was unusual to see quite so many paintings on the walls. Not that she had been in that many country homes of the nobility, but from what she had seen, the old estates like this often had tapestries hanging on the walls, not paintings. But they were lovely and it would provide a great deal of entertainment to wander about and admire the works.

"Later," Lady St. John said with a laugh as Caroline was about to become absorbed. "We ought to rejoin the others before Lady Worth announces supper."

Caroline conceded and followed her chaperone down to the main floor where a footman directed them to a different receiving room than where they had greeted the marchioness upon their arrival.

"It's a good thing there are so many servants about to provide direction or we'd be sure to get lost," Caroline said with a low laugh as another footman urged them along a different corridor.

"We'll soon know our way around," Lady St. John assured her.

Caroline again marveled at the other woman's change of attitude. Not that she had been terribly cold toward her up until now, but she certainly hadn't been this warm either. She didn't mean to distrust the older woman, but she was definitely curious about the about face. Perhaps the woman was just more comfortable in the country than in Town, she thought dismissively as they arrived to a lovely room that seemed very inviting to Caroline despite its vast size.

She supposed it was likely that all the rooms would seem vast in such a large house. And they didn't seem very full or crowded given their size even with the large number of guests, which Caroline thought was a good thing. It was one of the worst things about the Season, in her estimation, the *ton's* habit of cramming far too many people into their small houses. Even the grand houses of the upper echelons of the nobility couldn't comfortably allow for a spacious visit when they invited as many people as they could to each and every entertainment. It struck Caroline as exceedingly odd. She wondered if the nobles were afraid of silence.

A smile stretched her face at the thought. That wasn't a likely explanation considering they all owned these lovely, sprawling properties away from London. Surely there would be plenty of opportunities to hear the silence while they were there.

Caroline's father owned country properties as well, but he much preferred to spend his time near his banks and clerks and lawyers. All the better to count his money and ensure that he could make more of it. And so it was that Caroline was almost comfortable in Town and the country was almost a novelty for her. As she glanced around the lovely room, it struck her that perhaps marrying a noble wouldn't be so dreadful after all.

"Miss Smith, how nice to see you. I was afraid I wouldn't know a single soul."

Caro turned with a surprised smile. "Miss Nesbitt, I'm pleased to see you," she answered. She hadn't thought the other girl was so friendly on their first introduction, but she wouldn't argue with a pleasant welcome.

"Please, you must call me Samantha," the other girl continued. "If we're going to be together so many days on end, we cannot possibly keep calling each other Miss."

Caroline giggled along with the other young woman, feeling more carefree than usual. She actually couldn't have said when the last time was that she had genuinely laughed. It had surely been far too long.

"Thank you Samantha. And you must call me Caroline or Caro."

"Caro, I like that," the other girl replied promptly.

"Were your travels fine?" Caroline asked, unsure of the best way to ask the question.

Samantha grinned. "Fine is a good word for it. There wasn't really anything dire to complain about. It was long and boring but nothing dreadful like a broken wheel or anything like that happened, so fine is the exact right word."

Caroline returned her smile. "Us as well. I had forgotten how dull a long drive could be as I don't do it very often."

Samantha looked puzzled over Caroline's statement.

With a laugh, Caro added, "I suppose it is easy to block unpleasantness from our minds."

Samantha laughed along with her. "Since this is my first Season, I haven't actually done very much traveling before. Until recently, I had never been farther than a few miles from our house. My sister wed a few years ago, so we've travelled to visit her from home, but it is only a couple of hours drive." She shuddered before adding, "I'm only grateful that Chester Hill wasn't any further from Town than it is. As it is, it was manageable in one day since we got a good, early start."

"I suppose we could have put up at an inn or something if it had been further."

Samantha turned horrified eyes upon her. "I doubt my mother would have ever agreed to that."

Caroline stifled laughter. She didn't think it was unacceptable to stay at an inn. Surely the nobles did it regularly. How else could they travel far? She smoothed her face into as serene an expression as she could muster.

"I suppose it isn't anyone's first choice, but it would be better than missing out, surely," Caro finally answered. "While I have travelled more than you, it seems, I haven't had to stay at an inn either, so I really cannot say." She then turned the subject. "What has been the best thing you've enjoyed about the Season thus far?"

The other girl frowned as she pondered the question, forcing Caroline to again stifle her laughter. She hadn't thought it was a difficult question, but it seemed the other girl wasn't the brightest person she'd ever encountered. But Caroline had to appreciate her good nature and welcoming attitude. She couldn't disparage the other girl's intelligence just because it might not be sparkling.

"There are too many lovely things to pick just one, I'm afraid, Caro. Do you have a favorite?"

"As you said, there are so many." She had no desire to point out the other girl's deficiencies. "But I did particularly enjoy the breakfasts I was invited to. I preferred them because they weren't quite as much of a crush as most other events."

Samantha wrinkled her nose at Caroline. "You didn't enjoy the crowds?"

"Not particularly, I'm afraid. I found them to be a trifle stifling. Somehow, being in a crowd, especially in some of the ballrooms, made me feel a little bit as though I couldn't breathe."

"Oh dear, that doesn't sound pleasant."

Not wishing to bring a damper to their new friendship, Caroline pinned a smile in place. "It wouldn't seem we'll have that problem here, though, will we?"

Suddenly Caroline couldn't keep her attention on the conversation she was having, as a shiver climbed up her neck. Someone was watching her; she was certain of it.

Unsure if she ought to look around or try to ignore the sensation, Caroline made an effort to continue engaging the other debutante in conversation. Before she could think of what to say, though, the other woman turned the subject.

"He sure is a sight, isn't he?"

"Who?"

"The Honorable Mr. Northcott, that's who. He's the dreamiest man here. I wish he was hanging out for a wife, but rumour has it he doesn't intend to wed. I was nearly bowled over with my surprise when I found out he was a fellow guest."

Against her better judgment, Caroline's gaze followed that of her new friend toward the object of their discussion. She wondered if he had been the source of the tingle of being observed. Caro dismissed the thought as being ridiculous. As Samantha had said, the man was determined to remain single. And he certainly wouldn't be looking in her direction even if he had changed his mind on matrimony.

Or perhaps he had been observing Miss Nesbitt.

The thought wasn't entirely welcome, and Caroline felt the heat of embarrassment warming her cheeks, despite the fact that no one could possibly know what she had been thinking. Miss Nesbitt was her friend and the man was reputed to be a determined bachelor, so where he was looking really shouldn't matter. Nor her thoughts on the matter. But sometimes it seemed to her that the Northcott man's intelligent gaze could read her thoughts. Or at least that is what it had felt like when they had danced together. Perhaps her fanciful thoughts were getting away from her again.

Caroline was determined to rid herself of anything fanciful. Practicality was the best thing for her. She refused to consider going down the same road as her parents had. Any children she bore were going to feel completely comfortable in whatever life they chose for themselves. Or she'd die trying. The melodramatic thought brought a smile to her lips even as she turned her shoulder toward the handsome man.

Shivers of attraction would not keep her fed or secure, she reminded herself firmly.

Chapter Six

Gilbert's eyebrow twitched in its desire to lift in surprise, but he was determined to maintain his visage as neutral as possible. He couldn't believe the chit wanted to offer him the cut direct. Her companion certainly wasn't displaying such a vibe, he thought with a practiced grin as he sauntered toward them, despite Miss Smith's unwelcoming stance.

"Good evening. Neither of you look the worse for the wear of travelling down from London. Have you already been here a few days?"

Miss Nesbitt giggled, making Gilbert want to grit his teeth. He enjoyed feminine laughter for the most part, but this particular lady's amusement tended toward garish in his opinion.

"You are too kind, sir. I've just arrived this afternoon and so has Miss Smith. So it's highly pleasant of you not to remark upon the strain that is surely writ upon our faces."

"Not in the least, Miss Nesbitt," Gil declared in a flirtatious tone, careful not to roll his eyes as he bowed over her hand. When he turned toward Miss Smith to kiss her wrist as well, he was surprised to feel it clench as though she wished to form a fist, but then she relaxed into his hold and appeared indifferent. He couldn't help but admire her control. It would serve her well if his investigation turned up the worst.

Gil couldn't help thinking back to the many conversations he had argued with his overseer. Lord Chamberlain had been determined that Gilbert accept this assignment and hadn't much cared for his desire to avoid such a private social event.

"My lord, surely you must see that a man could end up married by the end of one of those parties."

"There are worse fates in life, Northcott."

"There might be, but I can't think of a single one."

Lord Chamberlain had laughed but had not relented. "It's not so bad, my boy. Are you not willing to make such a sacrifice as that for your king and country?"

"There are surely other agents who wouldn't actually consider it a sacrifice. Why cannot one of them take my place?"

"None of them could actually be countenanced by Lady Worth, surely you realize that, Northcott." The other man had been adamant. "And surely you aren't so daft as to be trying to convince me you couldn't accomplish this mission without compromising anyone."

Gil had been forced to grin over those words. The man wasn't wrong. Surely he could do so. It was a reflective impulse that made him wish to refuse the invitation. For the most part he refused to be involved in the social whirl of the Season. Only doing so enough to keep himself useful to his assignments within the Home Office.

As the younger son of an earl, one who had kept the success of his own financial ventures a well guarded secret, he was welcomed but not a brilliant catch. He was sufficiently pleasing that hostesses liked to invite him to fill out their required numbers. Just like his life as his father's spare heir, Gilbert hated being a place holder. So he had never accepted an invitation to a house party before. A part of him shied away from the thought of being that intimately associated with a group of people not related to him or one of his brother's friends.

Lucian, Gil's older brother, had always had friends around. He called them his kin. His friends and his four brothers were the most important thing in Lucian's life, at least up until his recently acquired wife. Far more important to Lucian than the earldom he was set to inherit. It had always boggled Gil's mind that his brother was so neglectful of his position. But perhaps it was because he had never had to. With Gil happily looking after all his duties, Lucian had been able to go about having adventures with his friends. It grated on every single one of Gilbert's nerves. But despite Gil's conflicted feelings about his brother, he had actually arranged for his brother to have a role at the Home Office.

A part of Gilbert acknowledged that it had been a way of having something over his brother. The fact that Lucian was Viscount Adelaide meant that he was limited in which missions he could take on. He was confined, for the most part, to watching over other members of Society rather than doing any real investigating.

Except for the investigation that had landed him in a situation where he gained a wife.

Lucian would have been better fit for this particular assignment, but since he was now on his wedding trip, there was nothing for it but for Gilbert to take over.

And that brought Gilbert back to his concerns over his own single state. Now that Lucian was married, it was even less likely that Gil would ever be called upon to inherit his father's earldom. All the more reason for him to take on real missions. Dangerous ones. Ones that didn't involve watching over some rich cit at a house party designed to marry off well dowered debutantes. The very thought made Gilbert restless and uneasy.

"If you cannot accept such a simple task, Northcott, how could you expect us to entrust you with the more complicated ones in the future?"

Gilbert felt all the blood recede from his brain for the briefest of moments before it slammed back in, bringing a massive headache with it.

"I beg your pardon, my lord?"

"I'm reasonably certain that you heard me, son." The other man had always been a mentor to Gilbert and obviously didn't want to hurt him.

"Are you saying that my position within the Home Office might hinge upon my acceptance of this assignment?"

Lord Chamberlain stared at him briefly as though wondering exactly how to answer the direct question. Finally he shrugged.

"We have to be able to know that we can rely on you for anything."

"Of course you can always rely on me, surely you should realize that."

The other man only continued to stare at him. Finally Gilbert bowed his head. There was nothing for it. He couldn't lose his position. It was the only thing that made him feel worthwhile.

"When do I leave?"

The older man clapped him on the shoulder. "I knew we could rely on you."

Even though it had been nearly a week since that conversation, Gilbert still fought the urge to slam his fist into any hard surface nearby. It was infuriating to find himself in the role of nursemaid. Or so it felt to him despite Lord Chamberlain's efforts to assure him that the investigation was vital to the safety of the nation. Gil nearly snorted at the thought. Roger Smith was a wily businessman but seemed loyal to his king, almost to a fault. Despite the fact that one of Mr. Smith's business associates was a known collaborator with one of the king's traitorous brothers didn't mean Mr. Smith had any involvement in their plots. But if the Home Office felt they had reason for suspicions and wanted him watched, then Gil would watch the man. And no one would be any the wiser.

And it didn't matter one single iota what the man's intelligent daughter might think of him, Gil reminded himself as he engaged the young woman and her friend in a frivolous conversation. It never ceased to amuse him when he fulfilled the role as a Society gadabout. Even his brother believed it about him, so well did he play the fool.

Casually looking around the room, Gil not so absently wondered where Mr. Smith was. If he had accompanied his daughter to the house party as expected, shouldn't he be with the gathered guests? Of course, being an older man, it was possible he needed more rest after his travels, and it was early days yet. Gilbert had fourteen days to get to know the man and decide whether or not the Home Office's concerns held any merit.

"Do you think so?"

Gilbert's stomach sank as he realized he hadn't been fully paying attention to the conversation. It was unlike him to lose track, even when he was being his social persona. Dragging his focus back to the matter at hand, he tried to recall what might have been said.

With a sly smile, he answered Miss Smith's question. "The theater isn't my favorite pastime, I'm afraid, so I don't have a truly educated comment on the subject. But I did think this year's presentation of School for Scandal was very well done, even though it has been done before."

Miss Smith appeared impressed by his recovery, as though she had been trying to call him out for his inattention. Gilbert looked upon her with renewed interest. Perhaps the next few days wouldn't be as dreadful as he had feared. But then he brought that line of thought to a full stop. He couldn't be intrigued by a woman. That was exactly the thing he had feared about attending a house party. With a quick shake of his head, he took his leave of the young women in order to approach another cluster of guests.

If he had to be there, he might as well take the time to get to know everyone. There was no way of knowing where he might be able to glean some useful bit of information the Office could use.

"We haven't yet been introduced, but since this is an informal gathering, I suppose we can get away without a proper introduction," he began as he approached his hostess' two grandchildren.

The young woman blushed, further revealing the inexperience Gil had suspected, while her brother bowed and stuck out his hand in greeting.

"Good evening, I am Bartholomew, Viscount Clair, and this is my sister, Lady Catherine Hannigan."

"Well there, that was nicely done, covering all the social niceties in one fell swoop," Gil answered jovially. "I'm pleased to make your acquaintance."

"I haven't bothered going about in Society until now, as I've expected it would be deadly dull. And my sister hasn't been introduced since we've been in mourning too many times lately. But Grandmother Worth deemed it was time, and she couldn't avoid it any longer, so I promised to keep her company."

Gilbert couldn't help but approve of the young man's sentiments and no nonsense demeanor. It would be a pleasure to spend time with him, especially if he could be himself rather than a Society fop. Gil resolved with a shrug that perhaps he could be somewhere in the middle for this country sojourn. He needn't be entirely foppish, but it was always an excellent shield for his investigations and couldn't be put aside completely.

"So you thought your grandmother's party would be the best place to start?" he asked the young woman.

Lady Catherine answered with a dimpled smile. "Grandmother thought her party would be the best place to start," she corrected. "I thought the best place to start would be running to the Highlands, but Grandmother Worth would have hunted me down and dragged me to Town by my ear were I to attempt something so lily-livered."

Gil laughed at her turn of phrase. "Well, I trust you will find she wasn't wrong."

"Oh, that was never in question. My grandmother is unacquainted with being wrong."

He liked these youngsters already and looked forward to watching their progress in the coming days. He would do all he could to help them enjoy their time in Society, even if he couldn't blame them for their aversion.

Speaking with the Worth grandchildren helped keep his mind off Miss Smith, but it still required more effort than it ought to keep his gaze from straying back toward her. It was odd because she wasn't beautiful in the traditional sense. Her hair had a reddish hue to it that he quite liked even though it wasn't considered fashionable. Gil wondered if she'd ever tried to alter the shade. He also wondered if she had a temper to match the fiery shade.

Suddenly, he felt his muscles and tendons stiffen slightly as though he were coming to attention. The object of his investigation had entered the room. No one looking at him would be able to tell that he had just turned into a stalker before their very eyes. Despite the hair on the back of his neck rising to attention, the rest of him remained lounged in the chair he had finally perched upon. Gilbert was proud of his ability to appear fashionable and bored even when he was about to pounce.

Of course, he doubted he would have to actually do anything particularly physical during this mission, which was probably part of the reason why he had been so opposed to it. He enjoyed the dangerous missions. They were what so set him apart from his brother. Viscount Adelaide could never be in the middle of anything even remotely thrilling.

Gilbert's obstinate desire to one up his brother was a source of amusement in the far reaches of his own mind. It was the one area in life that he knew he wasn't completely reasonable. He was also well aware that this one area probably coloured nearly all his other dealings. Including his determination to never be a place holder in company.

But, his presence at the house party was proof that all rules were made to be broken.

A slight frown flitted across his forehead. He was allowing his attention to be pulled in too many directions. Now that Smith was present, he would have to maintain his focus with an iron will, there was no other choice. He would never fail in a mission.

"Which of your grandmother's planned activities are you most looking forward to?" He finally realized that the conversation had lapsed slightly.

The siblings exchanged a glance before turning to him with a smile and answering in unison. "Riding."

Gilbert grinned and raised his eyebrows in question.

The young viscount answered him. "If this is your first time to Chester Hill and if you also like to ride, you are in for a real treat. Some of the best riding I've ever done has been here on our grandparents' estate. It is why Grandmother is hosting her party here rather than at Worth."

"Well, that, and the fact that this house is actually more suited to a house party than Worth." Lady Catherine turned to Gilbert with further explanation. "The royal suite takes up far more room than you'd expect and has to be always kept available. So there goes the opportunity for a few guest rooms. This place doesn't have a specifically designated Royal chamber, so there's room for several more guests. And it's large size will allow for comfortable entertainments whatever the weather." She paused and again exchanged a look with her brother. "But I do hope the weather remains fair and we can spend as much time as possible out of doors. I've been assured that when I finally go up to Town there won't be much opportunity for outside activities."

"Well, there is always riding in the Park."

"From what I've heard the crowds and the size of the Park are both rather disappointing."

Gil laughed at the girl's chagrined expression. "I suppose I shan't argue with you there. But if you can manage to rise early enough, the crowds aren't a factor and despite its smaller size, the paths in the Park are sufficiently enjoyable that you shouldn't have to hate it too dreadfully."

"Thank you, sir. I appreciate your vote of confidence."

"Not at all. I can understand anyone's aversion to city life even though I have for the most part chosen it for myself."

Gilbert laughed when the young woman faked a dramatic shiver of disgust over his life choices. If she only knew, he thought with an inner sigh. But still, he enjoyed the company of the young siblings. He could certainly respect people whose loyalty to family carried them to such lengths.

He turned his attention back to studiously ignoring the Smiths as he surveyed the rest of the room, much to the detriment of his investigation.

Chapter Seven

Caroline fought against her chagrin. How could the handsome man so ignore her? And why did she even care? He was a fop she insisted to herself, despite the evidence to the contrary. And not for her. She ought to be delighted that he wasn't paying court to her. It would make the next two weeks decidedly awkward if he did, as surely she could not accept his suit. The flutters he invariably caused in her midsection were unacceptable to someone determined to marry from her mind, not her heart.

She tried to steer her mind toward the purpose of their visit to Chester Hill. Getting herself suitably married. She tried to be discreet as she gazed about the room considering the possibilities.

There were several single, eligible gentlemen. Baron Crothers. Viscount Clair. Lord Thornwood. And Mr. Browne. She hadn't yet been introduced to their hostess' grandson, but of course Lady St. John had ensured that she knew who he was. Caroline didn't have any expectation of his pursuing her. Since he hadn't yet spent any amount of time in Town, it was unlikely he was in search for a wife. And if he was, he certainly wouldn't be looking to align himself with the likes of her.

Caroline shook herself from the negative thoughts. She was suitable and eligible. Lord Clair would be lucky to have her. But she did hope he didn't take an interest in her.

The baron was probably her best chance. Or Mr. Browne. She didn't know either gentleman well, but they had been introduced. Pleasant enough fellows. And with pockets to let. Quite perfect for her needs. And neither seemed the sort to profess undying, unbridled passion for her. Exactly what she was looking for. Never mind that her eyes still wanted to stray toward Mr. Northcott. Her eyes were fools and would lead her astray.

Very well. There were at least two eligible and potential partners present. She had two weeks. She could sit back and enjoy at least a few days of those weeks, surely, before she had to set her mind toward choosing who she ought to spend the rest of her life with.

Caroline only hoped her face didn't appear as grim as she felt as she turned back toward Lady St. John and tried to assure herself that she didn't actually have to accept either of those gentlemen if she didn't wish. She could even maintain her unwed state if she truly wanted. But Caro didn't think she had the fortitude for that choice. She would have to wed. But it was a daunting choice. The rest of one's life was a woefully long time.

Lady Worth approached and Caroline hoped she appeared pleasant and attentive as she dipped into a curtsey. She was a trifle nervous over the noblewoman's reception of her father. Caroline loved him dearly but understood how the nobles felt about his larger than usual personality.

"We're glad you could join us, Mr. Smith," Lady Worth said with a smile that even Caroline deemed genuine. Her respect for the marchioness grew.

"I was thrilled at the invitation," Papa said with his bold, deep voice filling the space around them. "My daughter, too. We haven't spent much time in the country in far too long. Of course, I'm not sure what I'll do with myself for two weeks without my ledgers, but when needs must."

He suddenly realized what he said and turned a slightly sheepish expression upon his daughter before turning back to their hostess.

"My apologies, my lady. I forgot I wasn't supposed to speak of ledgers."

Lady Worth laughed lightly and patted his hand. "Don't try to be something you're not for my sake, Mr. Smith. I'm sure we'll manage to keep you reasonably entertained so you don't miss them too terribly. Do you hunt?"

Mr. Smith grinned at the older woman and nodded. "Not often, but well."

And humble, too, Caroline thought with a smile.

"I'm certain Lord Worth will be happy to take you out, in that case. Also, your more analytical bent might enjoy billiards with some of the gentlemen."

She turned away leaving Caroline grateful that the older woman had tried to make her father feel included despite his less than acceptable social acumen. Caroline watched her father as he studied the other guests. She knew he was a shrewd judge of character. He had to be in order to be so successful in business. But he had a strange blind spot when it came to the *ton*. He so wanted to be accepted that he ignored any and all warning signs. Especially any warning signs in connection with his daughter's potential matrimonial partners.

It was going to be an interesting two weeks if nothing else.

Mr. Smith wandered away from them in search of less feminine conversation. Caroline wasn't sure if she was happy or disappointed to see him go. She worried for him in such an environment. Her father hated to feel wrong-footed. And he couldn't help but feel that way in the rarified company of High Society. Even though he might deal with gentlemen on an equal footing if one of them ever wanted to invest in one of his ventures, in a social setting of a *ton* event, it was all about one's birth, not one's accomplishments. Which was exactly why Caroline thought his desire to wed her to a noble was beyond foolish. Caro very much thought what one did with one's life was far more important than who gave you that life. No one could control which family they were born into. In her estimation it was ridiculous to set much store by it. And yet, here she was, obeying her father's edict and trying to snag a gentleman for herself. As long as she didn't fall in love with him, surely they could find a comfortable existence.

Her stomach started to feel queasy at the whirl of contradictory thoughts swarming through her mind. They weren't in the least bit helpful so she tried to dispel them. But in such a crowd and in company with her father, that was much easier said than done. She only hoped neither of them made a misstep that fortnight. Her father would be so disappointed.

"Miss Smith!" The overly jovial voice made her cringe.

"Lord Powell," she replied with little inflection as her heart sank. "I didn't know you were to be a fellow guest." She kept her gaze trained on the man's left shoulder in an effort to keep her true feelings from being displayed to all and sundry. Caroline couldn't believe Lady St. John hadn't warned her that the oily baron was to be one of the party. Perhaps she hadn't known. The queasy feelings Caroline was fighting intensified, and she feared she would not be able to partake of the coming meal.

"I was hoping you would be here, my dear," Lord Powell was continuing to gloat. "I asked Lady Worth especially, but she wasn't certain if you'd be able to attend."

Caroline had thought it had been Lady St. John's machinations that had gotten them invited, but perhaps she had been wrong. She swallowed the bile that threatened as her father returned to her side. Roger Smith would probably love the baron and his supercilious attitudes. Somehow the savvy businessman thought it right that the aristocratic Society look down upon his low birth. Caroline could barely tolerate it. Her chin rose along with her ire.

"Were your travels to Chester Hill pleasant, my lord?"

"Not in the least. The roads were dreadful and the inns were less than adequate. But we do what we must."

Caroline blinked, at a momentary loss for words. None of the other guests had such dire things to say about their travels whether they had been less than ideal or not. She stifled her sigh. His finicky complaints would probably appeal to her father. Caroline had to fight not to roll her eyes at the ridiculousness.

Why was Lord Powell the only gentleman who seemed interested in her? She couldn't even understand why he *was* interested. From the gossip, it didn't seem as though his pockets were to let, so he wasn't in desperate need of her dowry. And with her low station in Society, she would think he would look higher than her. While it was true that she was connected to the Callwell family through her mother, since neither she nor they acknowledged the connection, no one else seemed to do so either. And yet still, from her first event of the Season, Lord Powell had been the only one who consistently asked her to dance, called on her during Lady St. John's at home days, and invited her to go riding. It was unfortunate that he put her in mind of a toad.

Even his voice was a little croaky. But mostly it was his cold, and rather beady, eyes. Caroline felt a chill whenever he called on her. And when he asked her to dance, she always had to force herself not to allow her repulsion to show. She didn't want a reputation as a snob, but she just couldn't warm up to the man's attentions. And Caroline was afraid that his marked preference for her would discourage any other gentlemen from pursuing an interest in her.

She feared being stuck as Lady Powell for the rest of her days.

She ought to be grateful, she supposed. While she couldn't find him attractive, he didn't seem to be the sort who abused his animals or berated his servants, from what she could tell. That at least boded well. But he gave her the impression as though he wanted to possess her. As though he were a collector of pretty things, and he just wanted to add her to a shelf somewhere on his estate. She couldn't explain it any better than that and didn't really have a solid basis for her feelings. But he only ever watched her, and almost never asked her any questions. It seemed to Caroline as though he didn't much care what she thought on any given subject. So she couldn't possibly envision a future of partnership with the man.

Not that most noblemen would consider their wives to be their partners. But surely some must. She knew men of the lower orders would appreciate a wife as a helpmeet. Why couldn't her father see this?

It took effort to keep her thoughts from her face. And finally she allowed her eyes to flicker toward Mr. Northcott and she nearly startled when she realized he was observing them. Her chin lifted as her pride engaged along with her ire. She couldn't allow that man to feel pity for her even if she at times felt it for herself.

Thankfully, even though Caroline suspected that Lady St. John would be glad to be rid of the responsibility she had taken on toward her, the older woman wasn't as enamoured with Lord Powell's suit as Mr. Smith was, so while she didn't actively oppose it, she didn't encourage it either. Lady St. John cleared her throat.

"How good of you to greet us, my lord, but I see there are others we have not yet spoken with this evening. I am certain the same is true of you, we shall wish you *adieu* for now."

Clutching Caroline's elbow in order to ensure she accompanied her, Lady St. John swept away from both Lord Powell and Mr. Smith, who had returned to join them when he'd noticed with whom they were speaking. Caroline bit her lip to prevent her grin. The two men seemed to enjoy each other's company and barely noticed their departure.

"Be sure to speak with the other gentlemen as much as you can without being forward this week, my dear. It wouldn't do to allow anyone to think someone else has a prior claim upon you."

"No, of course not, thank you for the sound advice, my lady." Caroline hadn't needed that admonition, but she appreciated that they appeared to be in agreement on the topic, even if she would rather spend more time speaking with the other young women than the gentlemen. That was not the purpose of her debut into Society, she was very well aware.

Lady St. John stopped their stroll in front of the two gentlemen her charge had not yet spoken with. "Good evening, my lord, sir, might I preset my companion Miss Caroline Smith? Caroline, this is Viscount Clair and Mr. Browne."

Caroline dipped into an appropriately deep curtsey to greet their hostess' grandson and the other gentleman. Though she knew who they were, she had not yet been introduced.

"It's a pleasure to make your acquaintance, Miss Smith," the young viscount greeted. "Have you travelled far to be here for this visit?"

"Oh, not terribly far, just down from London like most, I'd say," she answered with a smile. "What about you?"

"We were coming from the opposite direction but not too terribly far, thank you. It was a pleasant day of travelling. It's a good thing that I don't mind my sister's company, though, because it was the first time we were ever confined together, just the two of us and her maid, for so long. If she had been prone to waterworks or sickness, it might have been an entirely different tale."

Caroline laughed along with the others even though she didn't find it all that hilarious. What if the man's sister hadn't been too fond of his company? Why was it the gentleman who took priority? She tried not to be so bourgeois in her thinking, knowing it wouldn't get her anywhere in the exalted company but she mentally scratched the young viscount off her list of potential suitors, not that he had seriously been on it in the first place. He was far too young for her taste, anyway. She would much prefer a more mature gentleman. From her estimation, a gentleman who hadn't yet gone out into the world couldn't possibly make a pleasant husband.

She turned to Mr. Browne, finding his warm hazel gaze to be approachable and appealing. "What of you, Mr. Browne? Did you come from London or from home?"

"Neither, actually, I was performing a commission for my mother that had me down at the coast for a time. So I might have had a bit farther to travel than most of you, but I managed it in two rather uneventful days."

"The coast must have been lovely at this time of the year."

"Indeed it was, Miss Smith. Have you visited Brighton in the fall?"

"No, only in the summer when it was absolutely stunning but a little overcrowded with everyone wishing to enjoy the cool breezes."

"Ah, yes, it has started to get quite fashionable now, hasn't it?"

Caroline smiled, amused to think she had ever been anywhere fashionable. She wouldn't disabuse the gentleman of the thought. She turned to Lord Clair again.

"Is there anything of note that you know your grandmother has planned for our visit?"

His eyebrow twitched in a curious way, but Caroline kept her focus on the gentleman's gaze.

"All manner of things such as riding and croquet and shuttlecock and archery." He paused for a moment. "Have you any experience with a bow and arrow, Miss Smith?"

"Not a great deal, my lord, but I have tried a time or two," she answered simply, not wanting to admit it was one of her favorite activities, as it was considered a trifle masculine for the fairer parties.

"I'll be able to help you, if you'd like. It's one of my best pastimes."

"How lovely," Caroline replied, unsure how to discretely extricate herself from a potentially awkward future encounter.

She was saved by the butler. Dinner was to be served in the green room. Caroline wondered why not say the dining room. *Perhaps with a house this size there are more than one?* When they reached the designated room, she stifled a grin. It was aptly named. She felt as though she were stepping into a forest, so green was the room. Every single surface was a shade of green. Various shades of green, in fact. Some of them were rather bilious. It was not her favorite room in the place, that was for certain. Would it suppress their appetites, she wondered, to be dining in such an overpowering chamber?

When she saw who she was seated next to, though, she had to fight hard not to allow her reaction to display itself upon her face. Caroline wished the marchioness had opted for the less formal as she had heard was sometimes the case at a house party. Instead, there was assigned seating. And she was to sit between Lord Powell and Mr. Northcott. If the room colours weren't going to affect her appetite, her dinner companions certainly would.

Squaring her shoulders to face the task as diligently as she could, Caroline smiled at Lady St. John, knowing the older woman would be aware of her discomfort even if she didn't agree with it completely. Lady St. John might not wish to encourage Lord Powell but Caro rather thought the other woman would think sitting next to Mr. Northcott was providential. The twinkle in the lady's eye made Caroline momentarily suspect that she might have actually had something to do with the place-card setting.

It took all her effort not to frown. That was the best she could manage when she first took her seat.

"Well isn't this fortuitous," Lord Powell declared, making Caro bite back a snort. Not in the least bit fortuitous from her perspective, but who was she to quibble?

Since she had already discussed their travels with each gentleman, Caroline wasn't sure which safe topics she ought to pursue even though she somehow felt the pressure of needing to start the conversation. She tried to assure herself it wasn't her assignment as she nodded to the footman who was filling her plate.

Whether she had an appetite or not, there was certainly plenty of food and it all smelled delicious. Caroline forced herself to taste a bit of everything and took slow calming breaths to quell the riot in her midsection.

"I would have to breathe through his attentions, if I were you, as well."

Caroline nearly dropped her fork.

"I beg your pardon?" She had heard him quite clearly even though Mr. Northcott had kept his voice low enough for only her to hear, but she was certain she must have imagined it.

He didn't repeat himself but looked at her with amusement dancing deep in his hazel gaze.

"Is this your first house party, Miss Smith?" He asked the question as though he were repeating it, making Caroline's lips twitch to keep her smile in bounds.

"It is, Mr. Northcott. Is my inexperience so evident?"

"Not at all. In fact, I only surmised it since this is your first Season. You have the air of an experienced hostess. So I would almost suspect you had presided over house parties of your own."

"Oh, that's kind of you to say, sir, thank you."

"Is it? I just thought it was truthful, not kind or unkind."

Caroline grinned at him, bringing a sheen of confusion to his eyes for a moment before he returned her smile. Caro redirected the conversation.

"What about you, Mr. Northcott? I suppose you've probably been to dozens of such parties."

"Why would you suppose that? Do I strike you as so very old?"

Caroline's eyebrows rose, and she blinked in surprise at both his words and his tone. It was as though he were somehow offended by her question.

"Not in the least. I would just expect that you would be considered a popular guest. And I expect you've probably been out in Society for a few years, so perhaps my calculations were off in guessing dozens but..." she trailed off with a slight frown of consternation. Caroline really had no idea why he would have taken exception to her statement. "My apologies, sir. I meant no offence."

"Of course, you didn't. No need to apologize. I ought to apologize to you. I am, perhaps, a trifle out of sorts from the long day of travel."

Caroline tilted her head to examine him more closely. He didn't look in the least bit fatigued. She was fairly sure he was stretching the truth about being tired and felt her curiosity climb higher about the man. Why would he be so prickly about attending house parties?

"In answer to your question, Miss Smith, I've only ever attended one other house party."

With her eyebrows reaching toward her hairline, Caroline expressed her surprise. "Lady Worth must be a particular friend, then, for you to finally accept an invitation."

"I'm flattered that you would assume it wasn't that I hadn't been invited."

Caroline was becoming increasingly confused by the man at her side. She wasn't sure if he was fishing for compliments or if he was trying to confuse her. And she didn't know how she was supposed to respond. Her blinking frown must have revealed her discomfort even as she tried to smooth out her concern because the gentleman at her side suddenly smiled and turned the subject.

"Since this is your first house party, have you any idea what to expect? I'm no expert, but I could probably advise you."

Having begun to think the handsome man might be slightly unhinged, she wasn't sure she wanted any advice he might have to offer, but she returned his smile and offered him a slight shrug.

"Lady St. John, who has far more experience than either of us, told me a fair bit about what I ought to expect. And she had the insider information of having discussed the matter at length with our hostess, so I think I'm fairly prepared, but I do thank you for your offer," she concluded, not wishing to seem ungrateful for his offer, even if she wished she could leave the uncomfortable situation she found herself in.

Mr. Northcott was nodding at her side and watching her face attentively as she spoke. Caroline suddenly found it appealing, as though he were actually paying attention to her words. It was uncommon amongst those she had met recently. Most assumed what you were going to say since everyone seemed to always say the same things. Caroline felt her smile turning more genuine as she met the gentleman's gaze. Until Lord Powell drew her attention back toward himself.

"You aren't eating much, my dear. It won't do to offend the cook on your first day."

Heat and discomfort climbed through Caroline as she fought against the urge to condemn the man's proprietary attitude toward her. She also wanted to repulse his suggestion that she was going to offend anyone, least of all the cook. Even if she wasn't eating much, how would the cook ever know that she hadn't eaten everything on her plate, she wondered. But as she was turning away from Mr. Northcott in order to address Lord Powell, their eyes met momentarily. The laughter and understanding that danced in the man's warm gaze made Caroline feel caressed for the briefest moment. This made her feel a trifle more prepared to deal with the weasel at her other side.

"I appreciate your concern, my lord, but I can assure you I am eating. It is just that Lady Worth has been so very generous in serving such delightful fare, and I cannot possibly hope to sleep tonight if I partake of it all."

"Nonsense, my dear. You could use a little bit more meat on your bones. How do you expect to bear healthy sons if you don't?"

These inappropriate words caused Caroline's face to flare with heat. Rage was the emotion she could identify, but it would seem the obtuse man thought he had embarrassed her.

"Perhaps I ought not to speak of something so delicate with a debutante, but it's the most natural thing in the world, you know."

Caroline opened her mouth to rebuke him but then couldn't think of what she could possibly say. She was relieved when Lady Catherine, who was seated on Lord Powell's left, drew his attention with a question about his horses. Caroline wasn't sure if the other woman had heard what he had said and was rescuing her or if she actually wanted to know about the animals, but she didn't rightly care. Her gratitude knew little in the way of bounds.

Turning her gaze to her plate, Caroline took a deep breath to steady her temper. How was she going to get through the coming days with Lord Powell present? At least she knew in her heart that she could never marry the man. She had been thinking it possible in order to please her father, but between Lady St. John's lack of enthusiasm and her own repulsed feelings, she knew it was no longer a possibility.

"You surely aren't allowing that buffoon to court you, are you?"

Her chin snapped up and her gaze clashed with Mr. Northcott's. "I do wonder how you think I could stop him."

"Have someone deny him entry to your parlour, for one thing."

"If you'll notice, sir, we aren't somewhere that I could even begin to lay claim to."

"No, I suppose not," the man agreed instantly with an awkward smile twisting his lips. "I misspoke due to my shock at the man's temerity."

Caroline stared at him in wonder despite his apology. Or maybe because of it. She was uncertain how to cope with the mercurial man. She had thought him rather frivolous and foppish but the intensity when he'd insisted that she not allow Lord Powell to court her had been anything but weak. It sent a strange thrill through her that she tried to ignore.

It seemed to her as though he were trying to restore his usual easy-going manner, but the watchful intensity in his gaze hadn't quite dissipated.

"Well, then, if Lady St. John is so informed, could you tell me what we ought to expect? How shall I be entertained in the coming days?"

Caroline somehow didn't believe he was being honest or genuine in that moment, but she couldn't very well accuse a man of playing a part. And in a way, why would it matter? Weren't they all playing roles of one sort or another? She tried to recall his question and answer it without sounding like an imbecile.

"There is to be music some nights and games of all sorts, as well as sports and riding and picnics and all sorts of the typical pursuits one would expect in the country. And dancing, of course," she added as an afterthought and was surprised to catch his watchful gaze once more.

"Will you save me a dance, Miss Smith?"

Caroline frowned. "I hardly think I need to keep a dance card at a house party, sir." She smiled, to show she meant no offence.

"You could still humour a man, couldn't you?"

There was nothing to do but laugh at that point. "Very well, Mr. Northcott, I'll be happy to dance with you when the time comes." And suddenly she found herself looking forward to their dance a great deal more than she knew she ought to.

Chapter Eight

G ilbert couldn't have explained what had gotten into him even if his life depended on it. He was supposed to be conducting an investigation, not reprimanding the girl for her choice of suitors. Not that it appeared that she had chosen the reprobate. *But what could those responsible for her possibly be thinking?* It made Gil think that perhaps there was some truth to the reason behind the investigation. He had thought it was all a hum. But if Mr. Smith thought Lord Powell was a good candidate for his daughter's hand then, at the very least, he was an imbecile. And the man's success in business assured Gilbert that wasn't the case, so there had to be a reason for his poor judgment in this matter.

It was one more thing he would have to look into.

Not that Gil had any intention of allowing the girl to get close to him, nor he to her, of course. But he couldn't in good conscience allow a sweet, innocent young woman to wind up in a lecherous man's clutches, even if her father was a traitor.

Not that he had any idea of how he could actually prevent such a misalliance, but he would have to make the effort. He had been surprised to see Lady Catherine intervene when Lord Powell was pestering Miss Smith.

It was almost as though she were being proprietary, but surely that couldn't be. Lord Powell was notorious. Gil doubted the powerful Worth family would allow one of their own to end up in his clutches.

But what did he know?

What he did know is that he needed to keep his focus centered on his investigation. As such, perhaps getting closer with the girl wouldn't be a bad thing. As long as he didn't allow himself to wind up in a compromising position, it should all be well. And really, the greater good would have to be applied in this situation. Gilbert would hate to cause the girl to have a misplaced expectation of his intentions, but if that happened, he would have to ignore his conscience. The good of King and Country would have to come before Miss Smith's feelings. He certainly couldn't wed every girl whose feelings were hurt, surely.

Of course, he could be completely inflating his own ego in this moment. Miss Smith hadn't previously displayed any indications of being inclined to have tender feelings toward him. Perhaps he had let his own fears be put out onto someone else. That would not do at all.

Turning to his right, Gilbert made an effort to engage Mrs. Nesbitt in conversation for a time.

"How is your father, dear boy?" the older woman asked in a rather strident voice.

"Very well, thank you for asking."

"He was such a rascal when he was young, wasn't he?"

Gilbert blinked, unable to hide his surprise over such an odd question. "I wouldn't know, ma'am," he finally answered. "He's always struck me as being very mature and serious, but I, of course, wouldn't have known him as a young man."

"No, of course not, I don't suppose you would. And losing your mother so young, I guess she couldn't have told you stories."

Gilbert knew etiquette dictated that he had to speak with the fellow guests on either side of him, but he was regretting the manners that had forced him to obey that unspoken edict. He was not enjoying Mrs. Nesbitt's conversation in the least. But as an agent of the Crown, surely he could manage to control one little conversation.

"It must be a challenge managing on your own without Mr. Nesbitt. I was sorry to hear of your loss."

"That is so very kind of you, Mr. Northcott," the woman shrilled, delighted to be on the receiving end of such weak sympathy. "It is, of course, a challenge, but my sweet Samantha is such a solace to me."

"Of course," Gilbert dutifully replied even though he refused to glance in the direction of the girl as Mrs. Nesbitt obviously intended. Clearly the fond mama was a matchmaker. But then Gilbert thought to use the woman to his own ends. "Since you're obviously an experienced member of the *ton*, what amusing anecdotes could you share about our fellow guests? I confess, I haven't been very actively involved with Society in recent years."

"In recent years," the woman repeated with a guffaw. "You try to make yourself sound old, Mr. Northcott."

"Not at all," he murmured. "But I don't have vast experience."

"Of course, you don't," she replied with aplomb as she gazed around the table and lowered her voice. "What would you like to know? All about the young ladies? Or the gentlemen's secrets?"

Gilbert forced a light laugh wondering if the nosy woman actually knew any of the men's secrets. He would play along with whatever she thought to share.

"There aren't any truly dreadful secrets to share with you, I'm afraid. It would seem Lady Worth has assembled a rather boring crop of guests this year," the bold woman began. "Mr. Browne has his pockets to let and that big house and all his little cousins to look after, so he's dangling after a wealthy wife. He'd do well to consider Miss Smith, but it isn't likely her father would want to allow it."

"Oh?" Gilbert didn't want to let on how happy he was that the woman had gotten to the heart of what he wanted to know on the very first try. He hadn't even had to lead her there.

"Thinks he can buy her a title, the foolish man. Surely he ought to know that no nobleman is going to want the likes of him muddying up their family tree. Not even younger sons with pockets to let."

Gilbert gritted his teeth. The woman was trying to stir the waters, that much was evident. And it didn't seem like she was going to be of any assistance to him. It was silly of him, but he was disappointed. There was nothing new in what the woman had to say. Judgmental tripe and something he already knew. It didn't take any digging at all to know the *ton* was dreadfully elitist.

"Do you have your eye on anyone in particular for your daughter?" he asked, assuming the woman didn't actually have anything useful to add to his investigation.

"Besides you, do you mean?"

Gil forced a laugh. He supposed he had let himself in for that with his question. He lifted his shoulder in a negligent shrug.

"My dear Samantha is young yet, so we're not in a real rush. And as I had mentioned, she is such a comfort to me. While I would expect to be included in her future household, I'm not quite ready to make such a transition, so I don't actually have my eye on anyone in particular."

"Why did she make her debut if you aren't thinking to marry her off?"

Mrs. Nesbitt shrugged. "Well, she was bored at home, and our mourning was over, so I thought why not?"

Gilbert suspected the woman was stretching the truth considerably. When one thought of the expense involved in launching a young woman's Season, he didn't think Nesbitts' pockets were so generously filled that they could do it frivolously. But if the woman wanted to appear less than desperate, who was he to call her on it? He smiled at her, keeping it as gentle as possible even though he could feel it wanting to turn slightly feral when her blinking turned owlish.

He tried not to be ridiculously arrogant, but he was well aware that women considered him appealing. Gilbert had used it to his own advantage many times. Being considered traditionally handsome had helped his investigations often. Except when he needed to remain forgettable. Then it took some effort. But Mrs. Nesbitt was no exception.

"Have you been enjoying the Season, then, as a more social venture than the hunt that some other mamas consider it?"

"Oh yes, far more exciting than sitting at home and thinking dour thoughts about my dearly departed."

Gilbert laughed lightly until he realized she hadn't been jesting.

"I can only imagine how difficult it must have been," he murmured before turning the subject. "What has been the best part about being in Town?" He was surprised that older women were the same as younger. He would have thought the mother would have a far different perspective on the Season than her child.

"The balls are the best, I should think. So many lovely gowns and dancers to admire. And the gossip. My favorite thing about the Season is finding out all the juicy tidbits about everyone," she declared with glee as she popped a bite of meat into her mouth with a grin.

Despite the fact that he himself took an unnatural interest in other people's affairs, he did it for a good reason, and it made him decidedly uncomfortable to hear the other woman taking such glee in having her nose in other people's goings on. He wished to end his conversation with her as it made him far too uncomfortable. He didn't like to think that his actions had any similarities to those of a busybody.

And really, he did need to be carrying on with his investigation. If he steeled his nerves, Gilbert was sure he could converse with Miss Smith without undue dire consequences. He had not stepped beyond the pale in their previous interaction despite her evident confusion with him.

"How did you enjoy the beef?" Gilbert could have bitten off his tongue over his untoward choice of conversation starters. Was he so very lacking in conversational ability? How had he ever thought he was a successful agent? He just managed not to shake his head in disgust at his own ineptitude.

"It was very tender," Miss Smith answered in a pleasant, but not effusive, tone, much to Gil's relief. He smiled and then had to work at not allowing the smile to deepen excessively when he saw the young woman's reaction. He could tell she wasn't sure what to make of him but still found him attractive. He could use that to his advantage. After she blinked and the moment stretched a little longer than it should have, she continued.

"The entire meal has been very nice. I am a little dismayed over not being able to do any of the dishes justice. But there is just so much of it. I would be unable to leave the table if I were to enjoy it as it deserves."

Gil was reassured that he wouldn't have to worry about her eating turning his stomach.

"Well, it's a comfort to know we shan't starve this week, at the very least."

Her tinkling laughter was pleasant to his ears and he was gratified to have been able to amuse her. "No, we certainly shan't." She paused for a moment with her head tilted in her curious way. "Of course, there is the possibility that the cook took some sort of bee in his bonnet and cooked up all the week's food into this one meal. In which case we will sorely regret not taking full advantage of each dish that passes us by."

Gilbert smiled at her droll words. "That would be a dilemma for certain."

"While highly unlikely, it would explain the excesses this night."

"Or they could be explained by the fact that we are at a marquis' favorite residence."

The girl laughed again and then nodded solemnly, struggling to pin a serious expression to her features. "That might be closer to the truth than my guess." She paused again before adding in a confiding tone, "The only other bad part about this meal is that it's making me think that I have been a dreadful hostess in the past. I have such an aversion to waste that now I fear I was inhospitable to our guests."

"Surely there can be a happy medium."

He was surprised to see the usually seemingly confident young woman appear uncertain. "I am sure there can be, but I don't know if I can claim to have achieved it in the past. I never heard any reports of complaints, but this has given me food for thought in any case."

"Why are you so averse to waste? Surely your father has more than enough that you needn't give it thought."

Suddenly the girl's expression was frowning and thoughtful. "I'd much rather use his wealth for good than to waste it in excess." She paused again, and he watched in fascination as she tried to straighten out her face and remove the frown. "But perhaps I've taken my aversion to waste a wee bit too far. As you said, there ought to be a happy medium. I will keep that in mind the next time we entertain."

Suddenly, Gil couldn't bear to see her downcast. "As you said, you have never heard complaints. You can be sure that you would have heard, probably through the servants, if anyone had been unhappy with what you served."

He was gratified by how relieved she appeared by his words. "You do make an excellent point, sir, thank you."

His stomach clenched though, as he watched her expression warm toward him. Gilbert realized that she had been quite reserved toward him until then, but suddenly her face looked more open and her gaze filled with curiosity. While it was what he needed to happen for his investigation, he was suddenly frightened about the outcome. He braced himself for what was to come.

"So what do you do, Mr. Northcott?"

"What do I do?" he repeated her question, at a loss, wondering if she somehow suspected something. He quickly dismissed the anxious thoughts.

"Yes, with your time," she explained, patient curiosity still coating her face and voice.

Gilbert was uncertain how to answer her. It was becoming evident to him that she wasn't an empty-headed young woman only interested in the next fashion plate. But he had his reputation as a Society fop to maintain. He would need to strike the right balance.

"I spend a great deal of time at my club," he finally answered, which was the truth. There was a surprising amount of information floating around the club.

She continued to look at him expectantly, as though knowing there surely must be more to him than that.

"I ride, I hunt, I practice various sports," he elaborated, fighting the flutter in his midsection when her face started to reveal her disappointment in him. She quickly smoothed out her face, but he could see that much of the warmth had left her gaze once more.

"Oh, yes, of course. Hunting is not my favorite pastime. Do you have a particular quarry that is your favorite?"

Gilbert was surprised by the question. A part of him liked all forms of hunting as it felt like good practice for his real vocation, but he couldn't rightly tell her that.

"Deer, I would say." He finally said the first animal that came to mind.

"Really?" she questioned. "I would have expected you to say something that would require a little more effort."

"Why is that?"

"It was just an impression I had of you, I suppose. I thought you would say peahens or partridge or something. Not that I think those birds are so very intelligent, but I would have thought they'd be a little more of a worthy adversary."

"I don't know anyone who would consider a partridge an adversary," he countered with a teasing smile.

She shrugged and blushed, evidently embarrassed by the interchange. "Perhaps I misspoke, but since they are a smaller target and so very easy to startle, I would think they would present a greater challenge."

"You are certainly correct in that assessment," Gilbert agreed. "I should be flattered that you think I would be up to the greater challenge."

Again her cheeks coloured, but she refused to be cowed. "Or I would have expected any young man to at least claim to prefer the challenge," she countered.

Gilbert laughed. He liked the girl's spirit. It was just too bad her father might be a traitor. Or she was. Or the both of them. What if the chit *was* the real culprit? It certainly didn't seem to be beyond her. She struck him as being remarkably intelligent for a young woman, especially a gently bred one. He didn't know many gentlewomen very well. He did know intelligent women. There were female agents of the Crown for whom he had a great deal of respect. But they were a different breed altogether.

Perhaps he was being an imbecile. He rather thought Miss Smith would think so. That thought forced him to stifle his grin.

He was just about to carry on in fruitless conversation with her when the marchioness stood to indicate the ladies were to leave the gentlemen to their port. Gilbert knew himself to be disappointed. He shook his head. This would not do. He ought be disappointed to lose a chance to question her, not sorry to lose her company. His smile was weak as Miss Smith took her leave. A part of him was glad to see the back of her. He needed to get his head straightened around. Surely the port would help.

He was losing his mind. He never drank on a mission. It would only lead to problems, not solutions, he reminded himself as he accepted the glass the footman held out to him. He would confine himself to a sip or two. He needed to keep his wits about him for certain.

It was exactly as he had feared. He had known full well that he ought to avoid the house party. But he would face any sacrifice for his position with the Home Office. Even if it meant being a foppish figure at Lady Worth's house party.

Glancing around as the other gentlemen were less discerning in their consumption, Gilbert thought now might be the time to learn something.

Mr. Smith and Lord Worth were debating the merits of coal powered trains. Gil's ears perked up. He hadn't expected the topic to drop right into his lap without his having to bring it up himself. He had to listen intently without appearing to do so.

It wasn't really a debate as it would appear both men were enamoured with the technology but couldn't accept that they could agree on anything. Gilbert was amused.

"Coal is the way of the future," Mr. Smith declared hotly.

"Of course it is," Lord Worth replied firmly.

"Doesn't coal make a dreadful mess, though?" Lord Thornwood asked gently. "Surely the people won't want that chugging through their fields and near their homes."

This brought both pairs of heated glares down upon his unsuspecting head, and Gilbert nearly laughed out loud at the put upon expression on the face of the young viscount.

"My dear boy, when the people see that they can get from Uxbridge to London in a few hours instead of a few days, they won't mind so terribly that there's a bit of dust left behind. Even driving behind a team of horses can be a bit of a dirty mess depending on the weather."

Lord Worth had begun his speech seemingly in a fit of anger but seemed much more reasonable and controlled by the end of it. Gilbert waited to see what Mr. Smith would say next.

"I do think you've seen reason," the old businessman said to his highborn host. "Have you already invested?"

Lord Worth's grin turned cunning. "Of course."

To Gilbert's surprise, rather than seeming offended that the marquis didn't appear interested in investing in one of his ventures, Roger Smith nodded in approval.

"Good for you. As long as it wasn't in Samuel Park's venture. That isn't going to lead to anything good. He doesn't have the right grade of steel. He's got a terrible accident waiting to happen on his hands."

"I could see that plain as the nose on your face," the marquis agreed promptly.

Gilbert took note of the name. Samuel Park was also under investigation from what he understood at the Home Office. Perhaps it was as he had suspected. Miss Smith could really be the saboteur, not her father. He wished for a moment that he could seek direction from Lord Chamberlain but dismissed the childish thought. He would have to continue his investigation with both possibilities in mind. Or rather his observations. *How could one really consider this an investigation,* he scoffed mentally.

Suddenly the footmen were bustling around refilling glasses and the two oldest members of the party appeared to be great chums. Gilbert blinked in surprise, unsure how it had taken place.

He supposed it had been Thornwood's question revealing to the two strong-willed men that they were actually on the same side of the issue. Gil wondered if it had been intentional on Thorn's side or if he had just blundered into the solution. It was hard to tell given the man's impassive features.

Gil was starting to feel like Worth and Smith would never end their chatter and allow them all to join the ladies. He tried to pay attention to their conversation as the subject usually interested him, besides the fact that he needed to know everything there was to know about Mr Roger Smith, but his heart just wasn't in it at the moment. He was surprised, though, when Lord Worth finally got to his feet indicating they could leave and rejoin the women. Lord Thornwood winked at him in a rather conspiratorial way, confusing Gilbert even further.

"Just like when we were in school and convincing the older boys not to fight with each other or one of us, eh, old chap. Although from what I remember, it was usually you who was the negotiator, never me. I can see why you liked the activity. It was quite exhilarating."

Gilbert stared at his childhood friend for a beat longer than necessary as he tried to decide if he thought Thorn was actually behaving suspiciously or if he himself were just becoming suspicious of everyone at the party since his investigation wasn't proceeding as quickly as he'd hoped.

He had never had reason to suspect Viscount Thornwood of anything. The man hadn't even cheated on a single test or exam as a boy. But people changed. His experience as an agent had certainly taught him that. Gilbert didn't expect anything dangerous to take place during the fortnight they were to spend at Chester Hill, but he had been slightly relieved when he'd seen that Thorn was present. Now he thought he'd have to keep an eye on the man rather than considering him a potential collaborator. Gil gave his head a slight shake. It changed nothing. He quickly left the room.

Chapter Nine

Caroline wasn't sure what to make of her father's joviality when the men joined the women who had been taking tea in the salon. He was usually so very serious that she liked to see him appear a little less uptight. But she had a strong tendency to fear the unknown. Her father in high spirits was most definitely an unknown. And him seemingly in the position of bosom bow to the Marquis of Worth? It was all Caro could do not to shudder at the potential for trouble over such a turn of events.

The ladies had all taken up various feminine pursuits while they sipped their tea, so there was a flutter of motion and activity as they all put away their needlework or paper and pencils.

Caroline had been trying to draw but wasn't satisfied with her results.

"That is quite a likeness." The deep, low voice behind her nearly made her drop her pencils, as she hadn't expected anyone to notice her.

Turning her head, she frowned a little before she could iron out the expression. It would seem Mr. Northcott managed to be everywhere at once.

"Do you think so?" she asked without inflection.

"You have an eye for details," he continued, making her face heat in delighted embarrassment. Caroline wasn't used to receiving compliments. It was delightful and awkward all at once.

"Thank you," she finally murmured. "Faces are not my forte, but our hostess' features are so unique, I couldn't help myself. Please, don't mention it."

"Your secret is safe with me," he returned promptly, causing strange flutters in her midsection, unused to feeling as though she shared a secret with someone. It made her feel warm in a most delicious way. Caroline tried to hold on to her reasonableness, but it was a challenge considering all the circumstances.

"Was your manly time as pleasant as it seems to have been for my father?"

Mr. Northcott's grin didn't really answer her question, but she quite liked how lighthearted he appeared to be.

"I wouldn't call it manly time, Miss Smith, but it was certainly entertaining."

Curiosity filled her at his words.

"It's a rather odd tradition, wouldn't you say?"

"For the ladies and gentlemen to go their separate ways for a time, do you mean?"

When she nodded, Mr. Northcott shrugged. "Not really. It wouldn't do to keep the gentlemen pent up for too long on their best behavior."

His words surprised a chuckle out of Caroline, and she warmed up to the man even more. She tried to keep a tight grip on her emotions, but there was just something about a good sense of humor that drew her in. *He's a fop*, she reminded herself determinedly, thinking of the impression he always gave her in Town. *But he doesn't seem to be nearly so foppish as usual*, the frivolous side of her mind whispered to her.

She couldn't argue with her own reasoning.

At previous events the man was often dressed in a far fussier manner than the women, which was really to say nearly excessively so. And he was always taking a pinch of snuff or waving about his handkerchief as a point of punctuation to his bored sounding pronouncements.

Caroline thought back to any previous interactions and couldn't say if his gaze had always seemed so watchful, as she had been too distracted by his antics. Perhaps that had been the point, she suddenly realized. Or perhaps she was just bored and reading far more into everything than she ought to.

"Why the sigh?" he asked as he finally took the seat next to her rather than hovering just behind her.

Caroline started. She had thought she had kept her disconsolate thoughts to herself. She tried to ignore his question.

"Lady Worth has mentioned playing a game of pantomime. Have you ever played?"

"Is that why you sighed, then? Are you not a very good actress?"

Caroline smiled at the questions, again ignoring the first one. "I've not actually had much chance to find out. As an only child, I didn't get much practice at some of things that others have a great deal of experience at. I suppose you and your brothers probably played it a great deal."

The gentleman shrugged. "Not really. None of us were much interested in anything played indoors. We have a tendency to associate this game with the sickroom, as we were always expected to entertain our brother if any ended up ill."

"Did that happen often?" Caroline was suddenly curious about his entire history. She hoped it wasn't a rude question.

"Not terribly often. Most of us were remarkably healthy. Our mother figured we'd all eaten enough dirt in our youth to ward off most ailments."

Caroline blinked, wondering if he were serious. "Your mother thought dirt was good medicine?"

The man's rich chuckle again caused flutters within her tummy, and she fought a squirm as she enjoyed it.

"Not exactly. I think she figured it toughened us up sufficiently, since it hadn't killed us."

Caroline laughed at that, seeing the reasoning, but then she sobered. "You mentioned most of you were remarkably healthy. Was there some of you who weren't?"

He quirked an eyebrow. "You do notice details, don't you?"

Caroline lifted one shoulder and smiled weakly, uncomfortable by his observation. "Details are important."

"That they are," he agreed promptly. "In answer to your question, I don't think any of us were exceptionally unhealthy, but the youngest brother did seem to catch more illnesses than the rest of us. It was he who made us improve our pantomime skills."

"So, you are good at it. I figured you would be."

Mr. Northcott seemed to study her for longer than was comfortable, and it crossed Caroline's mind that he wasn't at all the mindless fashion plate she had thought him. But before she could pursue the thought further, her attention was drawn across the room to where Lady Fanny was giggling along with something Caro's father had said.

Giggling wasn't anything Caroline thought she would ever witness Lady Fanny do, for one thing. For another, she had never witnessed her father inspire such a reaction in anyone, especially not a gently bred woman. She blinked rapidly, wondering if she had somehow slipped from reality, as her stomach pitched for the briefest moment. She swallowed down the adverse reaction and hoped no one else had noticed.

"It is a rather odd sight, isn't it?"

She should have known the no longer foppish Mr. Northcott would see everything at a glance. Caroline had no intention of discussing the matter.

"What is?"

"You don't feign ignorance very well, my dear," he said with a gentle smile, as though he approved of such a lack.

Caroline lifted a shoulder but didn't offer any other response. She suddenly wished the too perceptive man would just go away. She looked around the room to gauge what everyone else was doing. No one else except Lady Fanny's niece seemed to have taken an interest in that woman's interaction with Mr. Smith. It seemed to Caro as though most were caught up in their own interactions, not taking note of anyone else's. It was rather a curse to be so interested in the things going on around her, she thought with despair.

"Was it completely dreadful being an only child?" Mr. Northcott drew her attention back to himself.

Caroline forced a smile. "Probably not *completely* dreadful," she replied, trying for humour.

"I used to fantasize about it," the gentleman said, surprising a laugh out of her.

"Did you? I would have traded places with you in a heartbeat," she countered.

"I suppose we always think what others have is much better than our own, don't we?"

Caroline nodded. She often struggled with that. It was futile to wish she had been born a boy. Or that there had been a brother to grow up with. Or a sister. But a brother would have been much more satisfying for her father. Her eyes betrayed her by straying again toward where he was entertaining the ferocious but fashionable Lady Fanny. Could he be thinking to pursue a courtship of his own now that he was close to marrying off his only child? Did he think to finally produce the heir he had always wanted?

While a part of her assured herself that it would be good for him and she ought to be happy for him if he did, the rest of her quite repulsed at the thought of gaining a stepmother at her advanced age. Especially if the potential stepmother was one such as Lady Fanny.

She was getting way ahead of herself, she assured herself instantly and tried to drag her attention away.

"What made you think that being an only child would be an attractive state?" she thought to ask.

Mr. Northcott shrugged. "Not having to share toys with four other rough and tumble boys sounded quite luxurious in my young mind."

Caroline smiled. "I suppose sharing would have its disadvantages."

"But you can't imagine what they are?" he asked with a chuckle.

She joined him in laughter. "I would have given anything to be able to share the blame for things as a child."

"Ah, yes. Undivided parental attention would have had its drawbacks, I suppose."

"But you can't imagine them, am I right?" she asked with a laugh, imitating his earlier question to her.

Gilbert, Caroline wasn't sure when she had started to think of the handsome man by his given name. It was most unusual since she was never informal. Besides the fact that she hadn't ever heard anyone address him by it. But it felt right in her mind, and she failed to correct herself. Anyhow, Gilbert quirked a half smile at her question and shrugged.

"With five of us fairly close in age, it was a little competitive trying to gain our parents' attention. Especially our father who was so busy with running his estate and managing his lands besides taking his seat from time to time."

Caroline nodded. "I can certainly relate to having a preoccupied father," she answered with a smile that he returned, full of empathy.

"What of your mother?" Caroline asked quietly, fearing that she treaded on too personal territory considering his mother had already passed. She wasn't sure of the details or when his mother had died but she was reasonably sure it had been long ago.

"Our mother was lovely and we're certain she loved us very much, but she desired a daughter. From what I understand that desire killed her."

Caroline blinked at his words. "I beg your pardon."

"My apologies, Miss Smith. I ought not be melodramatic. But my mother died trying for more children. One would think five were enough for her, but she kept trying for a girl child."

Caroline's eyes prickled with the threat of tears, and her hand itched from an intense desire to reach out and pat his arm in comfort. It would probably be frowned upon. But she could so relate to his sentiments. Her mother too had died in childbirth, striving for the elusive heir.

"A common experience we share, Mr. Northcott," she finally managed to choke out.

"We have become a melancholy pair, have we not? And here we were to be discussing the upcoming game of pantomime."

Caroline appreciated his effort to lift the mood they had fallen into and forced a light laugh to correspond.

"I must warn you, sir, that I am deeply competitive at heart and am likely to make a great effort to win."

"I wouldn't have it any other way," he replied with a wide grin that did fascinating things to Caroline's midsection. They lapsed into companionable silence for a moment while surveying the others milling about. Gilbert interrupted her tumbling thoughts. "I really must ask, Miss Smith, even though we tried at first to ignore the strange occurrence, is there a relationship brewing between your father and Lady Fanny?"

Caroline felt heat staining her cheeks and collarbone. How was she to answer? She supposed the truth would do. "I am unaware of anything, sir, but it is a question I will be seeking an answer to as soon as I might discretely do so."

Gilbert laughed softly. "I probably should mind my own business, but I haven't ever heard friendly things about the woman, so it might be best if you did so sooner rather than later."

Feeling how tight her lips were, Caroline did her best to maintain a pleasant visage but was afraid she was failing miserably. She knew she shouldn't be offended or take the offensive in return, but she couldn't seem to help herself.

"Is it of any matter to you, sir? Are you hoping to throw a spoke into my father's plans if he were to have some?"

"With Lady Fanny?" his tone was incredulous. "Not at all. I just thought we were being friendly, and it seemed like a good idea to warn you a little, since you are newer to Town, you might not realize."

"Even if I'm from a small village, women are women, whether highborn or not," was all she bothered to say. With that, she was quite certain she had undone any goodwill she might have engendered with Mr. Northcott.

Chapter Ten

G ilbert wasn't exactly certain what she meant, but he appreciated that she hadn't overreacted to his inappropriate comment. He couldn't blame her for becoming cool toward him. He'd been a bit of a chawbacon. Really he was being completely inappropriate and that never happened to him. It was part of his personal identity. He had always played the role of responsible spare within his family. He never stepped out of line. He always did the right thing. Even his work for the Home Office was his way of doing the right thing even more directly. He felt as though he was able to do something good – something noble and powerful. What he could never do in his own life as the spare to his brother's inheritance. And even though this particular assignment felt a little odd and misplaced, he was going to do it with as much skill and wisdom as he possessed.

So what had he possibly been thinking to ask about Lady Fanny? It was beyond foolish to even imply to Miss Smith that he was more than slightly aware of her father.

He was only glad that she didn't seem to take note of the fact that it was odd of him to have noticed and even odder to have commented. But it was evident that it bothered her to see her father engrossed in conversation with the dragon-like older woman.

From an objective perspective, Gilbert supposed Lady Fanny was still attractive despite being past the first blush of youth. She had been widowed fairly young and had never had children of her own. She had been courted through the years by various noblemen from what he'd heard, but none had been brought up to scratch. He was surprised to see her cultivating a conversation with Mr. Smith. From the gossip he had occasionally overheard about the prickly woman, she set a high standard upon her own charms. But Gil supposed it was possible she had decided that she would rather pursue a wealthy man than a nobleman. It would be interesting to see how this played out.

But he was loath to stand by as a spectator if Miss Smith might be hurt in the process. Gil stifled his sigh and urged himself to leave the pretty young woman's side. He reminded himself he wasn't to stir up hopes in a debutante's heart. And he hadn't once asked her about her interest in industry. If he was going to investigate the woman he really ought to do so at some point.

The rest of the evening, including the promised game of pantomime, passed quickly. The next day, their hostess had a picnic planned near some old ruins the group was to explore. Gilbert had held himself back from spending too much time with any one fellow guest in order to observe them all and get a feel for the atmosphere that was to pervade the fortnight long house party.

It had been fascinating to say the least.

It was evident Lady Worth hoped to arrange matches. It was quite obvious to Gilbert which matches she hoped would take. He wasn't completely certain if she meant to match him up with one of her guests, but she was clearly relishing her role as matchmaker. He was surprised to see that she seemed to hope to match Miss Smith with her grandson. Gilbert liked to think he was as egalitarian as a son of an earl could manage, but he would have thought the marchioness would have had higher expectations for her grandson's wife. Perhaps she didn't so much care since the boy wasn't in direct line to inherit her husband's title.

But Lord Clair was just that – a boy – far too young to be taking on the responsibility of such an intelligent young woman. Not that Gil wished an empty-headed woman on the young man, but he was certain he wasn't going to be able to manage all that would be involved in marrying Miss Smith.

Not that it was any of his business, Gil reminded himself. And if his investigation led to what the Home Office suspected, then poor Miss Smith wouldn't be matching with anyone any time soon. Gil had to harden his heart not to feel badly about his role in that.

But he hadn't yet found any evidence that Roger Smith was anything other than a very rich cit. Gilbert might not enjoy the older man's raucous company overmuch, but he hadn't yet seen anything to make him think the man had anything treacherous in mind, even after a few days together.

He would have to search the man's rooms nearer the end of their stay. No matter what he found out through observation, that could always be wrong. There was also the possibility that the man had brought nothing incriminating with him despite Lord Chamberlain's conviction that the man was rotten. The Smith residences would also be searched during the two weeks that it could be guaranteed that neither Roger, nor his daughter, would be in residence.

Gilbert wished he had been given that assignment. He would far rather search all the man's homes, no matter how much travel or how dangerous it might be to break in, rather than playing his Society role in close quarters for two weeks.

But he had accepted the assignment. He really ought to stop whining about it, especially in his own mind. He was sure to sabotage his own efforts if he was being so negative about it.

The fine hairs on the back of his neck began to rise and suddenly Gilbert knew he was being observed. Allowing his eyes to sweep his surroundings, Gil was surprised to find Miss Smith frowning at him as she approached.

"Why are you following my father around?"

"I beg your pardon?"

"Why are you following my father around?" She repeated the words more slowly as though she thought he hadn't heard her clearly. He had definitely heard her. He just wasn't certain how to manage the question. His stomach clenched as his heart rate increased.

He tried to brazen it out.

"I have no idea what you are talking about."

"Yes, you do," she countered without even blinking, staring at him with accusation and curiosity clearly mixed in her gaze. Her frown deepened. "I would have thought it had something to do with his seeming friendship with Lady Fanny, since you asked me about it that first evening, but the manner in which you asked leads me to believe that it isn't something you would be jealous about. So then I thought perhaps you are trying to get him to let you invest in one of his ventures, but he told me you've never even asked to join one."

"Did you tell him you thought I was following him?"

For some reason, pink suddenly bloomed on her cheeks, and she shook her head slightly. "I did not. I thought it might be in my imagination at first. But I know that it's not. As you remarked previously, I notice details. I know I'm right on this matter. So I want to know why."

"I hate to contradict a lady but –"

"I'm not a lady," she interrupted him to counter. "So feel free to try. But I'll know you're lying to me."

Gilbert stiffened and drew himself up. "Northcotts do not lie," he scoffed.

She merely stared at him with one eyebrow elevated.

"Perhaps I am merely admiring his tailoring and didn't even realize I had been doing so." Gilbert altered his tactics. "I do apologize if I somehow made you uncomfortable."

She parted her lips on a breath as though she were about to speak, and Gil found himself holding his own breath wondering what she was about to say. He tried not to squirm as she scoured his face with her gaze. For the briefest moment he felt as though she could read all his secrets.

"I don't believe you. But I cannot prove anything, so I shall have to let it go for the time being. Just know, Mr. Northcott, that I will not stand for you doing anything that will hurt my father. He is a good man and deserves everyone's respect, not their disparagement."

Gil bowed to her. "I have meant your father no disrespect," he assured her earnestly.

She made a faint humming noise as though to dismiss his words. Gilbert felt a flush climbing his own cheeks. He had never been so embarrassed in all his days. No one had ever caught him before. And instead of an experienced fellow agent, it was this pretty little slip of a girl. He would never live it down if anyone were to find out, especially not one of his brothers or their friends. Gil clenched his jaw to prevent any foul language from erupting.

"Are you enjoying the explorations on this fine day?"

Gilbert tried to turn the subject. At first she merely stared at him in astonishment. But finally her face cleared and she smiled gently. It felt to Gilbert as though the sun had suddenly come out. Surely his brain had become addled on this assignment.

"I am enjoying it immensely." She turned her scrutiny away from him, finally, and looked around as all the well dressed people were clambering around the ruins. "It does seem like a strange occupation, but it is fascinating nonetheless. What of you, Mr. Northcott? Why are you not scurrying around with the rest of us?"

Gilbert wasn't sure how she had gone from being angry and accusatory back to being pleasant so quickly. He was well aware that women could be mercurial, but this seemed to be in excess. He grew even more suspicious of her. With her intelligence and evident acting skills, perhaps she truly was the traitor the Home Office was looking for. It made a strange sort of sense even though she was so young. He had seen stranger things in his time at the Office. He would have to continue to keep an eye on her as well as her father, he realized.

"I was just resting," he finally replied when her eyebrows started to rise in question. She didn't look convinced, and Gilbert realized he would have to improve his own acting skills if he was to successfully conclude his current assignment.

With a nod and half a smile, Caroline walked away, back to where she had been exploring before she came over to accost him with her accusations of watching her father. Gilbert swallowed his irritation. This assignment was turning out to be far more trouble than Lord Chamberlain had thought it to be.

Gilbert shrugged. It shouldn't matter. He was proud to serve. In fact, difficult should be all the better. It would be that much more satisfying when he concluded it successfully, he assured himself.

The ruins, he realized after he spent some time doing as their hostess had bade, were actually genuine. He had expected, when the excursion was proposed, that they were merely a folly as many of the noble estates had built around the nation. For some reason Gil couldn't quite fathom, the nobility was fascinated with the thought of archeology and so they had replicas of old, dilapidated buildings installed in sections of their land.

To him it was foolish on many levels. What was the sense of having a fake ruin? It would be of no use except as a novelty. But such was the vanity of the bored aristocrat. Some joined the Home Office and did something for their country. Others had fake ruins built in their spare property.

A grin split his face as he thought of the vagaries of his fellow man even as he continued to explore. It was still not his favorite pastime, he realized. He would far rather ride or play some sort of sport than to climb around a tumbling down old abbey. And the fact that it was genuine actually made it slightly more dangerous, as you couldn't be absolutely certain pieces wouldn't tumble down on you at any time.

He allowed his gaze to drift around again, verifying where Mr. Smith might be as well as who his daughter might be talking with. Gilbert nearly tripped as he caught Miss Smith watching him from the corner of her eyes.

It would seem he wasn't the only spy present, he thought with a grin.

Except that he was on the side of right, he assured himself firmly. It mattered little or nothing at all that she was a gently bred female. If she was trying to sabotage the progress of their great nation, she would have to be dealt with accordingly.

Gilbert knew Lord Chamberlain's sensibilities would be offended to know a lady was a guilty party. But he doubted the nobleman would actually be surprised. Nothing seemed to surprise the old coot. But Gilbert dreaded the task of having to tell him.

Get the evidence, he reminded himself, then telling his lordship wouldn't be so dreadful. Besides, there was a slim possibility that she was as innocent as a babe.

He turned his attention back to the pile of rocks that used to be some sort of Roman residence. Gil hadn't paid too close attention when Lady Worth had been explaining it since he had thought it was to be merely a fairytale. He was regretting his own arrogance. Apparently it wasn't only Everleigh that could boast genuine artifacts from that age.

"Mr. Northcott." Gil startled. Had he conjured their hostess with his thoughts? He turned with a smile.

"Good afternoon, my lady. I must say I am impressed with your magnificent pile."

The marchioness grinned. "It is a magnificent pile, isn't it? I am glad to hear you say so. I know your father is terribly proud of the ruins you have at Everleigh. I was interested to know your thoughts on ours."

Gilbert would never admit to the older woman what his initial thoughts had been, but he smiled politely. "I am afraid that I haven't fully educated myself on the subject of either our own ruins or yours. My father is far more fascinated with the subject as are a couple of my brothers."

Lady Worth made a humming sound. Gil wasn't sure if she was disappointed or merely acknowledging his words.

"But still, what do you think?" she persisted.

"I haven't yet had a chance to survey the entire site, of course, but I am impressed with the efforts that have been taken to clear the area without disturbing what remains. From what I understand, that isn't the norm. Usually people do one or the other – leave it to rot completely, or clear everything out."

The marchioness now nodded her approval of Gilbert's words. "Exactly, Mr. Northcott. Very astute observation. Worth has taken an interest in the ruins since he was a boy and insisted they be preserved as best as possible. It has been a task he has devoted many hours to."

"I look forward to learning more from him. I suppose I ought to have taken a greater interest in the rocks we have at Everleigh. But now that Adelaide is married, I suppose it's no longer my concern."

Lady Worth's smile turned sympathetic and Gilbert had to grit his teeth not to grimace. He didn't need anyone's sympathy. He wasn't going to be destitute, and he would have hated for something to happen to his brother only for him to inherit.

It had been a rather untenable situation to grow up in. Being raised as the spare heir led to an uncomfortable perception of your circumstances. Now that the heir was married, surely he would soon be producing heirs of his own.

Gilbert thought to speak to his brother about how he might go about raising any second sons without making them feel quite so disposable. But he didn't want anyone's sympathy. Least of all a lady who had ostensibly invited him to her party in order to round out her numbers. His jaw began to ache from the pressure he was exerting.

"Lord Worth would welcome your interest whatever the circumstances," the lady finally replied, ending the uncomfortable silence. "Do make sure you see the other side before we take our leave."

Drawing a deep breath after she left him, Gilbert had to admire the lady's hostess skills. He could see that she was taking the time to speak with every guest and ensure they were involved. An impressive feat considering she wasn't so young herself anymore and it was quite a large, uneven site.

He turned his attention back to his own task. He also needed to make sure he exchanged words with everyone. Gil needed to get back on track with that or he'd reach the end of the party and not have finished. That would be ludicrous considering how he'd scoffed over the fourteen-day assignment.

"What am I supposed to do for fourteen days?" he had demanded of his superiors when he was still trying to wiggle his way out of the assignment without actually declining it. *"Any investigating could be done in a day at most."*

"You don't know that, Mr. Northcott."

"My skills would be better served doing the searches, anyway," he had tried to insist.

"Mr. Northcott," Lord Chamberlain had begun in his booming voice. *"I do hope you aren't going to disappoint us."*

Gilbert had quailed at the very thought, as the man surely knew he would.

"You must know that not every agent, in fact very few agents, are in a position to be invited to such an event. You will have total access to Chester Hill. Anyone else would have to go as a servant. Far less access to the guests that way, as surely you realize. We are counting on you."

Gilbert tried to shake the memories. He ought not to keep reliving the uncomfortable experience. But he couldn't seem to get over it even though, or perhaps because, Lord Chamberlain hadn't been completely wrong.

He was starting to doubt if Mr. Smith was actually guilty of anything, least of all treason. But his superiors had been correct when they had insisted that he would need far more than a day to determine that. Especially in the environment of a house party, it was a challenge to question someone discretely without letting on that you were an agent for the Crown.

And apparently he wasn't being nearly as discreet as he had thought he was.

Again his eyes flickered in search of Miss Smith. And again he was surprised to note that even though she appeared to be engrossed in her examination of an ancient doorway, her gaze was drawn instantly to mesh with his as soon as his eyes landed upon her.

Gilbert wrenched his gaze away from her.

He needed to speak with others.

"Mr. Browne," he called out in as friendly a tone as he could manage. "What have you found so far?"

The other young man blinked and stared at him, evidently unsure how to answer the question.

"Well," he began, hesitantly. "I am reasonably sure I'm not the first one to traipse across these paths."

"No, no, I meant, have you come across anything that you've found particularly interesting?"

The other man's face smoothed out into a smile. "Well, if you enjoy old, falling down buildings, I'm pretty sure this is the best one out there."

Gilbert laughed and didn't bother to argue. He was convinced nothing could beat the ruins at Everleigh, but it wasn't worth saying so. He just shrugged. "I think builders could learn a great deal from examining the old ways. This building might be falling down now, but it stood for hundreds of years."

The other man appeared much struck by Gilbert's words, which Gil found heartily amusing. It wasn't a terribly revolutionary thought. But if you weren't involved in any construction projects, he supposed you might not have given it a moment's thought previously.

"Did your family live in a new house or an ancestral building when you were growing up?" Gil asked.

"We lived in one of my mother's father's properties. Very old. And cold and drafty. So my perspective of the old buildings might be a little influenced by that," Mr. Browne excused with a self-deprecating chuckle.

"Everleigh has been renovated many times over the last century, but I can relate to the drafts in some of the rooms," Gilbert agreed. "But I do love some of the design features in the old pile, even if I wouldn't necessarily want to be responsible for keeping it heated."

"I've heard Everleigh is spectacular," Mr. Browne commented.

"I'm partial, but you heard correctly."

They shared a laugh as they continued ambling around the old building, putting in time until the marchioness called them to the picnic. They could see the servants were already setting the tables up, so it wouldn't be much longer before they'd be called to eat. Gil was relieved as the breakfast had been a little too long ago for his comfort.

"I didn't hear you voice your opinion of the new railroads when we were discussing it the other evening, Browne. It seems all the rage to be backing some of those ventures." Gilbert complimented himself on the backhanded question as he awaited the gentleman's reply.

"I agreed with those who consider it the way of the future. I'm sure it won't be long before the tracks are crisscrossing the country. But I haven't backed any myself. All my funds are tied up in ore at the moment. Not as much promise of huge increases, but also little risk. I am not the adventurous sort," the man concluded with a self-deprecating smile.

With a nod Gilbert returned the man's smile. He didn't think the mild-mannered man hid any secret treasonous thoughts. He turned to see the others gathering and watched with interest as Miss Smith approached Lady Fanny's niece. Gil wished he could eavesdrop on that particular conversation whether it was part of his investigation or not.

Gilbert hadn't yet spoken many words with Lady Fanny's niece, Miss Brigham. She seemed pleasant enough, but it was hard to imagine being related to such an overbearing woman.

Chapter Eleven

Caroline could still feel the weight of Gilbert's gaze upon her. She ought to think of him in the more formal way, especially considering she was reasonably sure he was some sort of strange oddity to be watching her father so studiously. She wasn't sure if he was fascinated or repulsed as many aristocrats could be. But it was unnatural for him to pay so close attention to another man. It made her uncomfortable and awkward. But try as she might, she couldn't ignore him.

She tried to turn her attention to other things, but she seemed to always be aware of Gilbert Northcott. Perhaps he wasn't actually watching them and she was instead projecting her own interest onto him. That thought filled her with icy horror. And was why she had ended her confrontation with the man. If she had been wrong and he chose to make a spectacle of her, she was fairly certain she would die of the embarrassment. She made every effort to turn her thoughts elsewhere.

Another worry she had was the one Gilbert had pointed out. She had already been well aware of the strange attention Lady Fanny was giving to her father. It wasn't the first time a woman had pursued him. Being so very wealthy made him an attractive potential mate. Caroline had never noticed her father to pay the least bit of attention to the women who showed such interest. But Lady Fanny was different on many counts. For one thing, she was the first well-born woman to pursue him. Caro was afraid that his strange obsession with the *ton* would leave him open to being preyed upon by the dreadful woman. But she wasn't sure how to steer her father clear of the dragon lady.

"Good afternoon," she opened with a smile. "We haven't really had a chance to talk yet. I'm Caroline."

The other girl smiled, but Caro didn't really feel any warmth coming from the young woman. "I'm Karen Brigham."

"How are you enjoying the ruins?"

Karen's forehead crinkled and she lowered her voice and glanced around as though to ascertain whether or not anyone could hear her. "I shouldn't admit this, but I'm not really certain how I'm supposed to feel about them. I mean, I know Lady Worth brought us here with the expectation that this was a treat of no small order and others are quite delighted, so clearly I ought to be enraptured. But it's an old building that has fallen down. Why is this exciting?"

When Caroline laughed gently, the other woman smiled but then tried to frown her into seriousness. "If you repeat that I said that I will deny it completely."

"Your secret is safe with me," Caroline vowed. "I cannot say that I disagree with you, but I thought perhaps it was my bourgeois background making me feel that way, so you have relieved my mind somewhat."

Karen smiled and shrugged. "I'm not much less bourgeois than you, it's just that my father hasn't been as obscenely successful as yours, so it's considered somewhat more acceptable." She shrugged again. "Society can be foolish."

Caroline linked arms with the other young woman and started walking back toward where she knew Lady Worth was having the table set for the picnic. "I think we are to be quite good friends."

"I'm not so certain of that, Miss Smith," Karen cautioned, much to Caroline's shock. Her reaction must have been written on her features because the other woman was quick to continue. "It isn't that there's anything objectionable about you, but my aunt is a bit of a terror at the best of times, and I am fairly certain she has set her sights upon your father."

"And how would that interfere with our friendship?"

"It is obvious your father is an intelligent man. It isn't likely he will allow Fanny's pursuit of him to turn his head in the long run. She will be furious and will put an end to our friendship."

Caroline stopped and stared at the other woman. "Why do you suppose that might be?"

"She doesn't have any use for friends. She is only escorting me out of a sense of duty. And she sees me as useful as the need to escort me has been an excellent excuse for her to go where she wouldn't usually set foot. She is hoping to land another husband for herself, rather than really being interested in making a match for me."

"How do you feel about that?"

Karen shrugged. "I'm not much bothered by it, to be honest. I had very few illusions about her."

Caroline wasn't sure how to respond to the girl's words. "How does it come about that she is your chaperone? Is she truly your aunt?"

"She is, actually. She and my mother were sisters. Like you, my mother married beneath her station. Unlike you, her family didn't completely cast her off. But there isn't much family to speak of, just Aunt

Fanny, really. And she isn't in much of a position to sponsor me for another year, so I really need to make a match this year. Or she needs to wed someone with deep pockets."

Caroline was surprised at how frank the young woman was being with someone she had just met. Caro always found it difficult to open up to others, even those she'd known a long time. She wasn't sure what to do with these confidences. Especially the not so veiled one about deep pockets. She swallowed down her instinctive reaction. It wouldn't do to overreact to the older woman's pursuit of her father. As Karen had pointed out, it was most likely her father would see through the noblewoman's brazen pursuit.

Or he would finally be able to get that heir he had always wanted.

Maybe not. Caroline wasn't completely sure if Lady Fanny would be in a position to provide him with one. From what she understood, the woman hadn't had any children in her first marriage. And now she was older. She didn't have a completely clear understanding of such matters, but she rather thought it might not be possible. But still. It was an intriguing thought. Would she be more or less acceptable within Society if her father remarried?

It mattered very little. She was reasonably sure she was too old for a stepmother. It might have been a much better idea ten or more years ago. But her father had never seemed to be overly interested in pursuing the married state once more. He always claimed he had loved Caroline's mother far too much to consider wedding again. Caro suspected it was the thought of losing another wife that he couldn't face. And she couldn't rightly blame him. If he hadn't insisted so vociferously that she needed to find a husband, she would have preferred to remain at home with him for the rest of her days.

But here she was. At Lady Worth's house party. Staring at a very old building that had fallen down.

Suddenly a grin split her face.

"Tell me, Miss Brigham, about where you are from. And tell me, too, how you have enjoyed your Season thus far."

"So you are determined to ignore the threat of my aunt then?"

Caroline shrugged. "She might consider our friendship to be an asset, don't you think?"

Karen laughed, "I suppose she might." With that, she launched into speech and Caroline enjoyed the rest of the afternoon. They had sat together along with Miss Nesbitt for the luncheon. Lady Worth had not insisted on formality for the al fresco meal, so the three young women had chatted quite merrily. Caroline had thought they ought to have invited the marchioness' granddaughter to join them, but she had seemed pretty attached to her brother's side, so they hadn't bothered.

It was the best time Caroline had enjoyed yet that Season, and she was more than happy that Lady St. John had accepted the invitation. It would, of course, have been better if Mr. Northcott had not also been invited, but she supposed that was just the wee little fly in her ointment to keep her humble and not enjoying herself too awfully much. Her father had always insisted that you couldn't enjoy a thing too much or you'd never be happy again. Caro didn't completely agree with him, but who was she to argue?

Still, Mr. Northcott was being a very large fly. Caroline was beginning to suspect she wasn't going to be able to ignore the man much longer.

It was the third evening of the house party. There was to be dancing, and Mr. Northcott had bade her on that first day to save him a dance. The very thought led to an uncomfortable amount of shivering in her midsection. Caroline couldn't decide if she loved or hated the sensation. But there didn't seem to be anything she could do about it.

Having stared with a great deal of concentration at her reflection before descending to supper before the dance, Caroline was reasonably sure she looked as well as she could be expected to do. Her gown was of the highest fashion and her maid had done an excellent, intricate job with her hair. Too, the light green shade of the cloth seemed to be the exact shade to complement her complexion. Lady St. John had done well with her guidance. Caroline had always hated the reddish hue to her blonde hair but in the forgiving glow of the candles Lady Worth favoured, even Caro couldn't find much fault with her appearance.

If she was going to manage to attract a gentleman, tonight might very well be the night, she thought with a flutter of nervous excitement.

Who might it be? None of the gentlemen at the house party were dreadful, so that was a bonus. It was difficult for Caroline to consider that she might spend the rest of her days living with one of them, but she didn't think any of them had a propensity for beating their horses or servants, so it was unlikely they would beat their wife. Except maybe Lord Powell, she thought with a little shudder. Mr. Northcott had definitely not been wrong when he had tried to warn her away from the man.

The warning had certainly been unnecessary and somewhat embarrassing, but not wrong. If only some other woman would catch the man's eye. Caroline was instantly filled with guilt at the thought. She truly didn't wish ill upon any of the other young women, so she didn't really wish Lord Powell upon them, but she wished him far from her, that was certain.

He would probably expect to dance with her that night.

Caroline sighed. Always a fly in the ointment.

"You look beautiful, as always," Mr. Smith complimented his daughter as she joined him. "If only your mother was here to see you."

The prickle of tears threatened behind her eyes, and Caroline quickly blinked the moisture away. "You exaggerate, Papa."

"Not in the least. You've always been beautiful, but I've never seen you look quite this lovely. You'll break hearts tonight."

"That's slightly dreadful, Papa. I have no desire to do such a thing."

Mr. Smith rolled his eyes and then grinned at his daughter. "Are you ready?" he finally asked quietly, the first sincere interest he'd shown in her in an age, and the threat of tears returned to prickle Caroline's eyelids. She smiled widely to counteract the sensation.

"Ready," she repeated with a nod.

Her father put her hand through his elbow and patted it in place.

"Have you been enjoying your stay here?" Caroline asked her father quietly as they strolled down the stairs arm in arm.

"Somewhat," he replied with reservation. "Some of the people are far nicer than I had expected. And they're all more interesting than I thought they would be."

Caroline laughed softly. "It's always a surprise, isn't it?"

Her father patted her hand again, in good humour with his daughter.

"What of you, my dear? Have any of these fine gentlemen caught your fancy?"

Caroline was relieved that no one seemed to be in the vicinity to hear his not sufficiently hushed question. Heat crept into her cheeks, but she held her gaze steady upon his, not bothering to simper.

"Not yet," she admitted. "To be honest, I'm not even certain I wish to find a match, Papa. Why can't I just remain at home with you?"

"Because I shan't always be alive, and then where will you be? You know how dreadful it was when we lost your mother. I want you to have a whole family to help you bear it when you face another loss. You must have a husband, child. And I want grandchildren to spoil, too. Then you won't miss me when the time comes."

Caroline squeezed his arm to her side. "That will never be true." Despite his crass ways, she truly loved her father. She hated the thought of losing him but was much struck by the wisdom of his words. He had never used that argument in previous discussions on the topic. It was true, though. They were the only ones in their little family. If she didn't wed, she would one day be completely alone. That would be less than pleasant she was sure.

Unless he remarried.

"You could always arrange for some siblings for me."

"Now you're talking foolishness, child," her father scolded.

"So I don't need to look forward to having Lady Fanny as my stepmother?"

Roger's laughter was less than genteel but Caroline found it to be a relief. "That's quite unlikely, my dear," he finally said. Not a complete denial, but Caroline would have to be satisfied with it. They had arrived in the salon where the rest of the guests were gathered and there would be no more private speech that evening.

Moving into the room, Caroline joined her chaperone, Lady St. John, on a settee. While never far away from one another, Caro hadn't really spoken with the older woman much in the past couple days.

"Are you having a good time?" she asked Lady St. John in a low voice.

"Delightful, thank you, my dear. And you?"

Caroline appreciated the other woman's abbreviated style of speech. Except, of course, when she actually needed more information, but this evening it made her smile.

"I'm enjoying our visit here far more than I had expected," she admitted, keeping her voice low. It would not do to admit she had been dreading the sojourn in the country. "It is too bad we didn't bring Esther with us," she added. "I'm inclined to think it would have been a good experience for her to meet a few young ladies before her debut."

Lady St. John didn't comment, turning her face away and feigning that she didn't hear the end of Caroline's comment. She kept her sigh quiet, but Caroline was disappointed. It was not the first time it had happened. She wondered if the older woman would ever be completely open with her about why she was keeping the two girls so apart. If Caroline was such a dreadful influence, why had Lady St. John agreed to escort her? No one had refused to accept her, at least not superficially. Perhaps the highest sticklers hadn't invited her to some of their more private entertainments, but Caroline had never been given the cut direct, so she didn't understand why her hostess would be so determined to prevent her from befriending the lady's daughter.

It would have been diverting to be able to share her Season with a companion, Caroline thought with a touch of a sulk. She quickly dismissed the negative thought. It didn't matter. It was a kindness on Lady St. John's part to be escorting her at all. Caroline ought to be exceedingly grateful, even if she didn't consider Society to be the height of all that was good as her father did. She knew both her father and Lady St. John were doing what they thought was best for her.

If only she could agree with them, she thought with a disconsolate sense of despair sweeping through her for the briefest moment.

"My dear, please tell me you have not taken it personally," Lady St. John exclaimed softly beside her, bringing Caroline's attention back to her face. "If I had thought you wanted Esther's company so strongly, I would have considered it, but I didn't realize someone used to being the only child would miss it."

Caroline was surprised by her companion's words. She supposed she had never expressed herself clearly to the woman, so it was her own fault. Before she could begin to explain herself, though, Lady St. John continued in her soft, gentle voice.

"You surely noticed that my dear daughter hasn't yet matured to the point of being nearly ready for marriage. And while you are probably right that being here with us for this party would have benefited her, I was selfishly afraid she would be cast far too much in the shadow by your beauty and it might hurt her confidence further."

"Oh," Caro exclaimed. "I don't know what to say in response to that," she said with a light laugh. "I thought you didn't want her to be tainted by my company."

Lady St. John stared at her for a moment with a frown before she too laughed lightly. "Don't be a ninny, my dear. That's ridiculous, and I shan't even dignify it with an argument. But if you do not find someone to match with this Season, I will consider having her join us for some of the Season next year. As you said, she could use some polish."

Caroline was taken aback by her chaperone's words and further surprised by the fact that she then patted her hand and walked away as though she hadn't just altered her charge's perceptions of everything. Trying to refocus on the matters at hand, Caro allowed her gaze to travel around the room, and was again struck by Mr. Northcott's attentive gaze. It wasn't directed at her in that moment so she was able to watch him under her eyelashes.

She had noticed it several times. Gilbert Northcott was not the inattentive fop he would like everyone to think he was. But why would he want people to think that?

Once again she was convinced the man was observing her father far too closely. It was the strangest thing. Why would the aristocratic gentleman pay such close attention to the bourgeois cit? Caroline puzzled over the matter keeping a frown off her face with considerable effort. She had no desire to draw any more attention to the man's strange focus than was necessary. Hopefully no one else would notice. If Lady St. John thought she was a burden now, it would undoubtedly be far worse if there were any sort of brush with scandal.

All through the supper Caroline puzzled over the matter but could not come to any sort of conclusion. It made no sense. If Gilbert wanted to invest with her father, he could just speak to him. There was no need for studying him like a specimen.

And why would the man pretend to be silly when it was so evident he was not?

She finally had the opportunity to ask him.

Couples were forming for a country dance, and Gilbert had come to claim her.

"I think it's our turn, is it not?" he had asked her with an outstretched hand.

Caroline did her best to ignore the tingles that shot up her arm when she placed her hand in his. It was warm and strong and filled her with an inexplicable sense of security she had never before experienced.

She tried to harden her heart against the sensation.

"You are a curiosity, Mr. Northcott," she commented as they stepped toward one another in the routine of the dance. Her lips twitched as his eyebrows rose in surprise. It was beginning to amuse her that he tried so hard to be someone he wasn't. But it oughtn't, she reminded herself. Why would he do so? It sounded challenging.

"A curiosity, Miss Smith? I cannot say I have ever been accused of that particular thing before."

"Not to your face, perhaps," she agreed with a smile that clearly defied him.

His frown was becoming more evident, and Caroline wanted to giggle. She couldn't say why he would pretend to be a buffoon, but it was obvious to her that it was nothing but an act. For some reason, it made her like him all the more and no amount of heart hardening was going to help her attraction to the dratted man.

"Now *you* have become a curiosity, Miss Smith," Gilbert commented quietly. "I cannot fathom why you would think I am. I can assure you, I am the most average and boring man you are ever to meet."

"Now you are telling faradiddles," she accused with a smile. "Surely no one has ever accused you of being either average or boring."

The steps of the dance separated them for a time, and Caroline was surprised to see the man had himself well under control when he returned to her side.

"Did you enjoy today's activities?" he asked, turning the subject.

Caroline allowed the subject change as she really couldn't question him in the crowd of guests. If he were keeping secrets, that was really his affair, except where it pertained to her father. And that she couldn't demand information about while they were in company. She only hoped there would be an opportunity for quiet speech on the marrow.

"Today was delightful. I heard that tomorrow we are to go to explore the shops in the next village."

"That is what I have heard as well. Would you care to drive over with me in my curricle?"

It would be the perfect opportunity. They were likely to be far enough away from others to be able to have private speech, but out in the open so as not to be currying scandal in any way.

"I would like that very much, thank you." Caroline was delighted. While she still didn't think the earl's second son was actually considering courting her, she couldn't say that she would be disappointed if he did. Despite the fact that she found his behaviour strange and somewhat unsettling, the evidence of his intelligence was nearly as attractive as his overly handsome face.

Chapter Twelve

G ilbert knew himself for a fool.

While it would be good to have the privacy to gently question the girl about her father, the expression on her face revealed she was hopeful that his interest was genuine.

His interest was genuine all right. It just wasn't of the sort that a debutante would hope for. Gilbert had no intention of complicating his life with a wife. He wanted to continue his life as an agent for the Crown. It was unlikely the pampered and wealthy only daughter of a cit would be in the least bit interested in pursuing such a life with him. Not that he had any interest in complicating his life in any way, Gilbert reminded himself firmly. She was merely the means to the end of this particular assignment. As such, he would have to tread even more carefully. She was obviously not unintelligent. And if she turned out to be the saboteur he was searching for, his interest would be all the more pointed but unpleasant for her.

He breathed a sigh of relief when their dance came to an end.

And then he sighed in disgust as Lord Powell swept her up into the next dance. Gilbert couldn't understand why Lady Worth would have invited such a bounder to her party in the first place. Unless Mr. Smith had asked her to. Not that Gilbert thought the older woman would cater to anyone's dictates but her husband's. He remembered with a start that his own invitation had likely been at the demand of someone, so perhaps it was possible that the lady *could* be influenced. What a complicated mess.

When Gil's gaze shifted to watching Mr. Smith's reaction to his daughter dancing with the nobleman, though, it didn't appear as though he were all that enamoured with the situation. His expression was stoic at best. Gilbert was sure the successful businessman was well able to hide his reactions. He wouldn't have been nearly so successful if he couldn't, but Gil didn't think Caroline's father was terribly anxious to see his daughter become the next Lady Powell.

Gil turned his attention back to his investigation. So far he couldn't find any connection with any of the guests. None seemed exceedingly interested in the industries that the Office considered threatened. In fact, Lord Worth had seemed to be the one showing the most interest in it, and he was clearly above accusation in this case. Or so the Home Office had concluded.

He had never held such complicated feelings about an assignment before. He had found himself in various situations, some more dangerous, some far more boring, and he had never before wanted to quit. But somehow, this house party just might be the death of him.

Giving his head a slight shake, Gil admonished himself. It was probably his own negative view that was sabotaging his efforts. He hadn't wanted to come from the very beginning and was likely causing his own prophecy to come true. That would not do at all. If he was an investigator, he was supposed to be at least somewhat neutral. He shouldn't assume anything, least of all that he was going to have a dreadful time.

And it was time for him to get on with his investigation. The Smiths might be the main focus of his investigation and he was not assigned to search their properties, but he had been sent to this house party for a reason. He planned to search everyone's rooms. And while everyone was preoccupied with the ball would be an ideal time.

As an eligible bachelor, he couldn't absent himself for long without being missed by someone, but surely he could slip away and see what he could see. In his experience, criminals weren't always the brightest flames ever. It was entirely possible incriminating evidence might actually be lying about in one of the guest chambers.

He hurried through the female guest wing first but a quick listen at each door indicated that his guess had been correct – there were too many servants about. He hoped he hadn't completely miscalculated and would be able to search the gentlemen's rooms at least. Even though Roger Smith was his primary assigned target, Gilbert wouldn't rest easy until he had fully investigated everyone. Since it was suspected that he might be doing something clandestine at the house party, it stood to reason someone else was involved as well.

Things finally started to seem like they were going his way and he was able to take at least a cursory glance through each of the visiting men's rooms. However, nothing was obvious and glaring in identifying any one of his fellow guests as someone intent on damaging any fledgling industries.

It was disappointing. But he hadn't truly expected anything so obvious to fall into his lap as it were. And now he would have a baseline of what the rooms looked like for when he found time to search again more thoroughly. At least of the men's rooms. He would have to hope for the best with the women's.

A clock chimed the hour somewhere in the distance, and Gilbert realized he had been gone longer than he ought. He hurried to return to the ballroom, hoping he could brazen it out if anyone remarked upon his absence.

To his chagrin combined with relief it seemed that no one had taken note.

Casting his gaze around at his fellow guests, he realized everyone was enjoying themselves. While Gilbert was certain no one would be able to tell that he wasn't, there was really no reason for him not to be enjoying himself, too. Since he was there to look into Roger Smith, that should actually be making it all the more interesting. His fellow guests were, for the most part, pleasant and kind. Their hostess was being generous. He was being a dead bore, and that could not be acceptable. Gil could only imagine what his mother would have had to say to him if she were ever to know.

Of course, she never would. Not the least because she was no longer with them. But also because Gil was so readily able to hide what he was really thinking.

Or was he?

~~~

"Could you please give me an honest answer as to why you are taking such a keen interest in my father?"

Gilbert nearly drove his horses off the road with her question.

"I beg your pardon," he said as a means to buy himself some time. The only response he got from her was a tinkle of laughter. Gilbert turned to her with elevated eyebrows and what he hoped was a sufficiently arrogant expression to cow her into changing the subject.

"You said the same thing the last time I asked you. But I believed you more then than I do now. And that isn't very much." Her tone was dry, but there was still laughter in her voice. "Mr. Northcott, really, you needn't look at me as though you think I'm something lower than the dirt under your shoes. I know you are very good at feigning things. You are certainly not the empty-headed fop you'd like Society to think you. So I don't think you're nearly as surprised by my question as you are currently trying to make me believe." She took a deep breath, and Gil had a momentary reprieve before she continued, keeping her voice so low that even he could barely hear her. "You have been watching my father in the strangest way. Like you're studying him. I know it can't be because you are considering going into some sort of joint venture or you would just ask him outright. So why are you always staring at my father?"

Gilbert opened his mouth as though to protest, but she cut him off.

"Don't bother trying to claim you have no idea what I'm talking about. I would prefer not to involve anyone else, but I will if you aren't honest with me."

Gilbert stared straight ahead through his horse's ears, trying to decide what would be best. It was evident the girl could be discreet, but how could he possibly confide in her? Did he really have a choice whether he wanted to or not? Weighing all his options, Gilbert nodded in decision.

"There has been some suspicion that your father might be involved in a plot to carry out industrial espionage."

There was a beat of silence before she laughed right out loud. It was the happiest sound Gilbert had ever heard, but it didn't last long as she quickly stifled the volume. She didn't stop laughing right away until she was watching him carefully with a frown upon her face. Her laughter died completely when she suddenly asked:

"Are you serious? Or do you have that much control over your face? I can't really tell while looking at you from the side," she explained while her voice still sounded full of amusement. "You cannot possibly be serious, though, because there is no way anyone would consider my father capable of espionage, let alone willing to participate in something so heinous." She chuckled again as though Gil had told her a jest. "I mean, really, who could possibly think something so ludicrous? My father has made what is considered an obscene amount of wealth from his interests in industry. How could anyone suspect him of being involved in bringing that industry down? Do they think he has somehow converted from being a man driven by a love of profit to someone suddenly consumed by philosophy?"

When Gilbert didn't reply quickly she lapsed into what was evidently a stunned silence for a beat or two.

"You are serious. But that's ridiculous. You've met my father. You cannot possibly agree with this strange suspicion, can you? I had begun to think you were more intelligent than you let on, but I can see that I was mistaken. Have you had a fever recently?"

Gilbert felt his heart flutter slightly over the genuine kindness in her tone as she asked her last question. The girl actually sounded concerned for him despite the belief that he was wrong. But of course, he couldn't expect her to believe the suspicions about her father. Now he would have to find a way to control what she did with the information he had just imparted. Before he could do so, though, she had begun to speak again.

"So you're telling me that you have been watching my father these past few days in an effort to ascertain whether or not he is involved in some sort of plot or scheme, is that correct?"

Gil reluctantly nodded.

"What did you think you would see? Did you think he was likely to announce it? Did you think he had lost all discretion along with his mind? I cannot even begin to fathom who would have been so wrongheaded as to start you upon this quest."

Gilbert had to laugh over her wording. She wasn't wrong in thinking it was unlikely that he would make such an announcement.

"I had thought I was being sufficiently discreet that no one would be the wiser, for one thing."

The girl laughed, surprising Gilbert with her pleasant disposition once more.

"Most wouldn't have noticed." Her kind tone didn't reassure Gilbert. It was as though she were consoling a small child. But it was a bit of a comfort when she added, "I have always been more attentive to details than most. It can be both a blessing and a curse. But I would have to say that whoever sent you on this errand really ought to pay much more attention to details than they have. I mean, really, how could anyone in their right mind consider my father likely to be involved in such a thing?" She scoffed again before adding, "It isn't that I'm trying to say my father wouldn't be capable. I'm sure he would be. He probably knows many unsavory individuals who could help him carry out a plot of some sort. What I'm saying is that there is no reason why he would. Roger Smith is notorious or famous, depending upon your perspective, for his love of innovation. He has invested all his time and most of his money into every possible invention and venture people could come up with. To think that he would turn around and sabotage any of it is illogical. And besides that, he is a loyal servant to His Majesty, the King. I am assuming you must be an agent of some sort, so that is probably a factor in some sort of reasoning. Sabotage is a big word and a terrible accusation. The Crown is sure to be involved. But that is one more reason why I know my father isn't."

She laughed again and shook her head. "I'm sorry that you have been sent on such a senseless mission. Are you terribly disappointed?"

Gilbert smiled. He was amazed at her reaction. She didn't appear angry or offended in the least. Instead, she was concerned for his well being. He supposed that was a product of her conviction. She was so sure of her father's innocence that she didn't need to be concerned about the investigation at all. It put a small chink in his own conviction.

"I am not disappointed as I have not yet concluded my investigation." He didn't bother telling her that she was also a suspect. He wondered briefly how she would react to that information.

Silence followed his statement. He turned to look at her for a moment. She was staring at him as though he had lost his mind. But then her face softened.

"Are you new to your work?" she asked. "How does someone become involved in an investigation like this? I would probably be quite good at it, but I don't suppose they invite women. I'm rather surprised they would invite such a wellborn gentleman." She paused again and then answered her own question. "Then again, I don't suppose just anyone could mingle in a setting like this. But again, I must ask what you actually thought to discover in such a setting?"

Gilbert sighed. "I had much the same argument, to be honest."

Again the young woman laughed lightly. "Well, at least you will be able to show them you knew better."

"What makes you so sure, Miss Smith?"

"Oh surely, if you are becoming intimately acquainted with my father by investigating him, we ought to be on a first name basis. You must call me Caroline. Or Caro, if you'd like to be friendly."

Gilbert was appalled at the suggestion. It was bad enough he had been forced into admitting to her that he was investigating her father, but he couldn't compound that by becoming overly familiar with her. Even if the thought of being friendly caused an inexplicable flutter in his stomach. He ignored the ridiculous sensation. No doubt there had been something off in the breakfast.

"Miss Smith," he began with a touch of emphasis. "You must realize that these things take time. I have not concluded my investigation. It is entirely possible that there is an entire realm of things you don't know about your father."

She actually shrugged as though she hadn't a care in the world.

"I am sure you are right. It is quite likely there are things a man wouldn't want his daughter to know about him. But I do know my father loves money. He loves money, then he loves me, then he loves our king and country. Whatever else there might be to know about my father, these three things are absolute facts about him. And sabotage of any part of any industry would not be compatible with these facts." She paused and stared at him for another beat before adding, "So, that means you are investigating in the wrong direction. But I'm reasonably sure my father could help. He knows everyone. If there is anyone involved in any sort of sabotage, Papa would know who to suspect. You ought to ask him."

Gilbert laughed. "I cannot ask the subject of an investigation to get involved." Nor was he going to tell her that he was becoming suspicious of everyone.

"Well, if you want to find your culprit, it would be the wise thing to do," she argued.

"Do *you* know everyone there is to know?" Gilbert suddenly asked, causing her to still all motion while she stared at him.

"Are you thinking to involve me?" She sounded both incredulous and intrigued. Gilbert shrugged and nodded.

"I can see that you are convinced of your father's innocence. If you want to help prove it, there is no better way than to help me find another viable suspect."

She blinked at him in stunned silence before she nodded slowly. "I still cannot comprehend how anyone thought Papa was a viable suspect, but I can see why you would say that I might be able to help." She wrinkled her nose suddenly. "But is this not decidedly bad *ton*? I mean, how would Society feel if they were to discover that we were doing so?"

"All the more reason to help me quickly so we can be done and have it behind us and we'd avoid any possible scandal associated with your own name."

"If it were to be discovered that my father was under investigation, it is likely that I would be ruined anyway, isn't it?" Suddenly, she wasn't so full of laughter as she turned a fierce glare upon him.

"I have no intention of allowing you to be ruined," Gil insisted.

"Mr. Northcott," she began in exaggerated patience. "I am far from the most intelligent creature. If I was able to tell you were showing too much interest in my father, you can be sure others have noticed as well. In fact, I'm quite surprised my father hasn't confronted you yet. He would be the first to notice such a strange thing."

"It would seem you *are* the most intelligent creature present at this house party for I can assure you, you are the only one who has noticed."

She gave a low hum as though she didn't agree but didn't want to say so aloud.

"The thing is, if we were in Town, I'd be far more able to help you. There is no one unsavory here." She stopped for a moment and laughed lightly. "Or rather, I should say, no one of this particular type of unsavory – no one who would be up to this sort of thing. Even if I were to try to help you, there isn't anything to be done here at Chester Hill."

"You can't know that for certain," he insisted.

"I hate to so rudely contradict you, but I'm sure that I can know that for certain even if you can't accept that. I will give thought to who you might wish to interview in Town. Perhaps you could send a message to someone else and they could look into some other, much more likely people."

Gilbert wanted to stare at her, but he still had to drive his pair of horses. While they were even tempered and well behaved, they had never been in this area before, and he couldn't just leave them to their own intentions. But he deeply wished to interrogate the pretty young woman at his side. He needed to remove all adjectives that pertained to her from his mind, he admonished himself. She was now the subject of an investigation as well as a reluctant assistant. He couldn't have any sort of descriptive thoughts about her. It would be best if he had no thoughts about her except in connection with this investigation.

And she was busily telling him he was being completely wrong-headed.

He couldn't even argue with her.

It was most disheartening.

Chapter Thirteen

Caroline pinned her practiced Society smile to her lips and held it there. She couldn't allow the man at her side to realize that he had injured her in any way. In multiple ways, if she were perfectly honest with herself. For one, she had actually allowed herself the foolish inclination of thinking he might be interested in her in a romantic sense. It turned out he actually thought she might be tied up with her father in a criminal adventure of some sort. As if! Foolish man. But clearly he wasn't romantically inclined.

And how could he possibly think either she or her father were caught up in anything that could be considered espionage or in any way threaten their beloved industries? That was beyond foolishness.

Despite her smile, she felt a deep sigh welling up from within, and she had to swallow hard to keep it down where it belonged. She would never admit that he had injured her.

Of course, she would now have to help him. If left to his own devices, he would be all sorts of wrong. And probably ruin her while he was at it. And if there were any truth to the suspicion that there was some sort of plot underway, she would have to help him figure it out, as it could not be allowed to go forward.

But why, in the name of all that was holy, would they even begin to suspect her father?

Caro sat and thought on the subject for several moments, missing the beauty of the passing countryside until a sudden idea occurred to her and it took all her concerted effort not to gasp from the surprise.

"I bet it's one of my father's competitors," she blurted out but kept her voice low.

"What is?"

The man was rightly puzzled as she had essentially thought out loud. Caroline's smiled grew more genuine.

"Whoever gave you the crazy idea that my father could do something so foolish. It was probably one of my father's competitors starting a rumour. They do that all the time. It's the worst thing about business, in my estimation."

Gilbert's stare was torn as he shifted his gaze between her and the road repeatedly.

"You think it's just a rumour," he repeated.

Caroline shrugged. "Have you actually seen any true evidence that there is some sort of nefarious plot afoot?"

"There is always a nefarious plot afoot," he said.

She blinked in surprise, but then rallied. "That may well be, but have you seen any evidence about this particular plot?"

"I have, yes, unfortunately."

"And it pointed to my father directly?" Caroline frowned. She knew it couldn't be so. But how was she to prove such a thing? The very thought threatened to overwhelm her even as a sliver of hope contributed to her joy. Perhaps she would no longer be eligible for the

Society wedding her father wished for her if he was under investigation for sabotage. Not that she actually relished the thought of being ruined. But if there were to be a bright side to look at, she would happily take it.

"Not exactly directly. But close enough," Gilbert replied, making Caroline's frown deepen. That was vague enough to give her concern.

"Sounds like you might be grasping at straws, then. Or someone is. There is no reason to believe my father could be involved in something like this, and it's a terrible waste of your time if there really is some sort of plot underway. You ought to be elsewhere looking into someone else."

"I would think the families of most plotters would feel similarly."

Caroline nearly fell out of her seat, so great was her shock. It was requiring greater and greater effort to keep herself from overreacting and causing a scene. While she wouldn't mind returning home and resuming her comfortable life there, she didn't want to be the cause of her own downfall. And really, if she couldn't prove Mr. Northcott wrong, social ruination might be the least of her concerns. It was entirely possible all of her father's hard won assets could be seized in the event of his being arrested for something nefarious. Perhaps that could be the motivation behind all this.

She tried to keep the glare off her face but suspected she wasn't successful when his eyebrows rose. "Is the government hoping to seize all my father's wealth? Is that what is behind this ridiculous investigation? Because I'll have you know, he employs very intelligent and experienced lawyers to protect himself from this sort of thing. I can assure you, you will not be successful."

It relieved her slightly to see that he was shocked by her accusation.

"This is not a plot against your father, Miss Smith. He is under suspicion. There is cause for that suspicion. Valid cause."

"Why won't you tell me what that cause is?"

His exasperated sigh could have parted her hair if it wasn't already well tied down by her maid's many pins. "He has been known to associate with men who have been proven to be involved with the plot that we know for certain is underway. The extent of your father's involvement is the only thing under investigation at this time."

Silence fell between them for a moment as Caroline processed his words.

"So what you are telling me is that someone or multiple someones are trying to sabotage industries in our great nation." She waited for his nod before she continued. "Can you tell me which industries? Is it the trains? That would be so heart-breaking. Why would anyone want to sabotage any industry? What is in it for them? I mean, I can sort of understand wanting to sabotage a competitor in order to get ahead. I wouldn't agree with such an underhanded action, but I can see how someone might think that was justified or something. But that's not what you've said, is it? And that would be easy enough to investigate or prove. And wouldn't involve the Crown."

"You are far more knowledgeable than most debutantes, Miss Smith."

His grudging comment made her grin.

"That shouldn't surprise you, Mr. Northcott, considering that so are you. I mean, more knowledgeable than most gentlemen."

He bowed his head slightly in acknowledgement of her words but before she could carry on with her speculation he interrupted her thoughts.

"We're nearly to our destination. I'm sure I don't have to repeat to you how very silent you must remain on this topic. It would be to both of our detriments if this information were to get bandied about."

"I know how to keep a secret," she answered a trifle huffily, making him smile in amusement.

"See that you do. We will have to continue this conversation later."

"You can be sure that we will," she replied with a frown, wishing he wasn't right. But she could see that the marchioness' carriage was turning into an inn yard. Caroline supposed this was where they were to take their luncheon. She wasn't sure if she would be able to swallow a single bite.

What a disappointment this drive had turned out to be, she thought disconsolately as she tried to keep her features smooth and unconcerned. It had been beyond foolish of her to allow herself to think Mr. Northcott had developed feelings for her. How had she allowed her imagination to run so far away on her? She usually prided herself on being calm and level headed and not in the least bit imaginative. This was proof positive of why those were such good qualities to cultivate. She tried to remind herself that she didn't want a love match anyway and someone who was conducting wrong-headed investigations couldn't possibly be a good match for her, but she wasn't in the mood for that much logic.

When Gilbert lifted her down from the high perch of his carriage, Caroline tried valiantly not to feel the warm press of his hands on her waist. And she certainly ignored the sensation that he was lingering in the process. Surely that was just an odd trick of the angle of the sun, she assured herself as she also told herself that the shivers she was experiencing were due to the fact that she was actually more hungry than she had realized. The heat that stained her cheeks by the time he finally unhanded her had only to do with her anger over the conversation.

Caroline had to fight not to roll her eyes at her own foolishness even as she hurried away from Gilbert's unsettling presence. She wondered if it would be remarked upon if she rearranged the driving arrangements for the trip back to Chester Hill even as she sought out one of her friends. Of course, she couldn't do that, as they had to finish their discussion. But for now she was to have a reprieve.

That was the best part about the house party.

Caroline had found it difficult to make many friends during the Season thus far. Even though, as her friend Amelia had pointed out early in the Season before she went off and married Gilbert's brother, each lady only needed one gentleman, it felt to Caro as though each of the debutantes were in competition with one another. And it really felt as though some of the other young ladies held it against her that she had certain advantages. But her only advantages were of the financial sort. She didn't have any supportive family to smooth the way for her. All she had was Lady St. John.

A sense of disloyalty swept through her. Lady St. John had done her best, Caroline was sure. It couldn't be helped that the dear woman was just doing her duty. Caroline had never felt like someone's duty before and it was not much to her liking. But it ought to be viewed as a kindness that the woman actually felt so duty-bound to her childhood friend's memory that she would be chaperoning that old friend's daughter in the Season in her place. And she truly had been making an effort to set Caroline at ease. So, in fact, there was no "only" about it, Caroline lifted her chin on the thought. Having Lady St. John on her side was an asset she was determined to be proud of.

Caroline had thought her father had pressed upon that long ago memory and forced the woman's hand. Caro was sure her father meant well, but it was beyond embarrassing to think she had been foisted upon someone when she was used to being popular and liked in her own right. But perhaps she had been mistaken. It was evident Lady St. John held very vivid, warm memories of Caroline's mother and had transferred at least some of that affection upon Caroline herself.

In their small village, even though she wasn't high *ton*, she was considered gentry and thus well accepted. Not so much in the rarified environs of the Season. Now she had to rely upon Lady St. John's connections. And the kindness of Lady Worth. It disconcerted Caroline, but she was determined to brighten her attitude.

That thought led Caroline to join the marchioness as she was directing her guests expertly.

"You are such a skilled hostess, my lady. I admire the ease in which you keep everyone in line," Caroline complimented.

Lady Worth smiled. "Having had a large family helps with that, my dear. You'll see."

"Well, I'm not sure about that, but I do hope to see. Coming from such a very small family, I do think it would be lovely even if I feel as though I won't know how to go on in that environment."

"Don't turn missish on me now, Miss Smith. You strike me as a very efficient, knowledgeable young woman who will have no problems adjusting to whatever life throws at her."

Caroline stared at the older woman. "I think that's quite the nicest compliment anyone has handed me, thank you."

Lady Worth returned her smile. "It's much easier to compliment your gown or hair, but those are simply trappings, aren't they my dear?"

Caroline felt the threat of tears, surprised to feel so understood by this kind, older woman. She couldn't come up with an answer, so she merely offered her assistance. "It appears you have all well in hand, but is there anything I can do to help?"

"That's kind of you, thank you. It is all well in hand, as you said, but I'm afraid my granddaughter might be allowing herself to remain far too much in her brother's shadow. Would you mind trying to draw her out a little bit?" This last bit was uttered in a confiding whisper and thrilled Caroline all the way to her toes. Feeling as though she had a mission to accomplish that did not entail investigating her father filled her with renewed zest and purpose.

"It will be my pleasure."

It was a challenge ignoring Gilbert and all they had discussed, but Caroline managed to successfully push the thoughts to the back of her mind for the time being. She would wait and see if the marchioness rearranged the rides for the drive back to Chester Hill. Caro didn't have it in her to campaign for it on her own. Her intention was to avoid scandal, not court it.

The young woman she approached seemed to welcome her interest even though her eyes kept darting back toward her brother. Caroline knew the girl was young. Perhaps she was just a little too young for Society yet.

"Do you get to visit your grandmother often?" Caroline asked. "This is such a beautiful area. I'm pleased to have finally gotten to see it."

"We don't come here very often. We visit her at Worth on occasion. And she, of course, visits us."

Caroline nodded even though she didn't understand. Why would they not visit often? She supposed there were drawbacks to having family, such as feuds and misunderstandings. Just look at her own situation. She ought to have a large welcoming family but since they had disowned her mother, it was as though they did not exist or rather that she did not exist. It was fortunate for her that Society in general hadn't really noticed or it would have ruined any chance she had.

"I suppose it would have been a challenge for your parents to travel with small children when you were young. It probably became a habit for your grandmother to come to you rather than the other way around," Caroline said, even though she was fairly certain it was a common practice to send children to their grandparents for visitations.

"Our mother never liked to be parted from us," the young woman added with a small smile.

"And now your father is probably missing you as well."

"He has reassured us that he can handle two weeks."

"Why did he not come with you if he was so dreading the separation?"

Caroline knew as soon as the question left her lips that she shouldn't have asked it. But it was already out, and she had to live with it. She kept a pleasant smile on her lips and hoped they could brazen through the experience.

The younger woman stared at her with wide eyes and just shrugged.

After a couple of beats, Caroline determined to try again. "Will you be making your curtsey next Season?"

"It has not yet been decided," the girl replied with an apologetic smile.

Caroline was concerned for her extreme shyness. Or perhaps it wasn't shyness. But there was clearly something amiss. Her curiosity was piqued, but she wasn't comfortable prying. She hoped the girl would be able to overcome her reticence. Or her mother might be the problem, she thought with a frown.

"Did your mother regale you with stories of her come out? My mother passed when I was much younger than you, so I didn't get to hear very many of hers. I'm sure they would be highly diverting."

"My mother said the only good thing that came of her Season was meeting my father."

"Ah, I see." And Caroline did see. It was evident the marchioness' daughter had not enjoyed Society and had passed that fear to her daughter. She would have to mention it to Lady Worth. In the meantime, she would try some other tactic.

"What is the best thing about where you live?"

The young girl stared at her as though she couldn't comprehend the question, and Caroline sighed a little even though she kept her smile pinned in place. Her neck prickled and she was fairly certain Gilbert was watching her. It added an extra layer of pressure onto her wish to succeed with the girl. She added an extra dose of warmth to her smile and tried to explain herself.

"I usually live with my father in Somerset except when he has to travel to Town. Which is actually rather frequently, but that's a digression. Really, we probably more accurately live in London and visit Somerset. But I prefer our house in Somerset, so let us say that is where I live." Caroline laughed and fidgeted with the fabric of her gown before carrying on. "Anyhow, the best thing about our house in Somerset is our neighbours.

Everyone is lovely and I've known them my entire life. We visit one another and share meals and know each other's affairs. It is the closest thing to family that I have, and I miss them terribly even though we write every week and they keep me up to date on all the news. The second best thing is my horses. Because we ride everywhere when we are visiting each other, we have quite a large stable, probably more horses than we ought to have, but I miss them terribly and worry that they are eating themselves fat while I'm not there to see to them."

Finally, the lady joined Caroline in laughter and seemed to relax for the first time since they'd met, much to Caro's relief as she was unsure how many more silly anecdotes she would be able to come up with in an effort to make the other girl comfortable.

"I see what you mean, Miss Smith," she began in a gentle voice once her laughter died down. "The best thing about where we live is our dogs, I think. They are the most loyal and energetic companions anyone could ever ask for. They never talk back, they are never cross, and they always think I am the very best thing they have ever seen."

"Oh, how lovely. What sort of dogs do you have?"

The girl wrinkled her nose. "I'm not sure that they really have a sort. They are large and brown and their coats are about a medium length. The housekeeper complains about their hair falling out all over the place, but they are just so lovely that we cannot reprimand them even if they do get on the furniture at times."

"They sound delightful. I have never had a dog, as my mother was afraid of them so my father never allowed them in the house. There are some, of course, that work with the sheep, but they have a job to do and haven't been terribly interested in making friends with me." Caroline was pleased when her new friend laughed

154

over her small jest. "There are cats, of course, to protect the house from small intruders, but they are rather haughty and don't care to make friends, either."

"Oh no, cats are never the sort to be friends," the girl agreed. They shared a grin and lapsed into companionable silence for a time before the girl finally spoke up. "Are you enjoying being a debutante? You do seem to be having a lovely time. Perhaps it isn't so dreadful as my mother thought?"

Caroline's heart shrank for the sweet young woman beside her. "I am quite sure you will be highly successful as a debutante. But it is good that you are getting a little bit of practice here with your grandmother. The first few gatherings you attend, if they are large ones, especially, can be most overwhelming if you haven't been introduced to large events before. Not that this event is so very large, but at least there is likely to be one or two people with whom you've already become acquainted so it shan't feel as though you are facing a large sea of strangers."

"Oh no, that would be dreadful."

"Do you go to assemblies and such in your village?"

"No."

Caroline blinked, unsure how to proceed. "That would be a good place to practice, as well. If the only gentleman you've ever danced with is your brother, you might be less experienced than you'd like when you get to your first ball."

"Is it terribly uncomfortable dancing with a stranger?" the girl nearly whispered the question, making Caroline have to incline her head toward her to hear.

"Not any more uncomfortable than dancing with someone you know," Caroline answered with a gentle laugh. "It all depends on the partner, to be honest. If he has clammy hands and doesn't know where to put his feet, even if he's your closest male friend, it won't be very enjoyable. But if he is skilled at the dance and knows how to take the lead, it is one of the most thrilling experiences I've yet had."

Lady Catherine stared at her with wide eyes, searching as though for the veracity of Caroline's words.

"Really? More thrilling than racing your horses?"

Caroline laughed. "Hard to believe, I know, but yes, a good dance partner can actually be more thrilling than a great horse in certain contexts. Your horse will probably be more loyal, though," she concluded with a wink, making the other girl grin and reach out and clasp her hand.

"Thank you ever so much, Miss Smith. You have alleviated my worries, at least somewhat."

"We shall stay in touch. I look forward to hearing all your successes during your Season."

The other girl didn't look completely convinced about that but smiled anyway.

There was a bustle of activity once everyone had completed their nuncheon before heading out to the shops. Lady Catherine, after a brief and quiet goodbye, went to join her brother. Lady Worth surprised Caroline by beckoning her to her side.

"Thank you my dear. That appeared to be successful. Might I ask you how you drew the girl out of her shell?"

Caroline's heart went out to her noble hostess as she seemed genuinely concerned for her granddaughter. She offered the marchioness a gentle smile.

"I think she is hungry for attention, and we were able to find a common ground."

"I thought you might find you have much in common with you having both lost your mothers quite young. I know you were even younger than my poor girl when my daughter died, but the fact that your mothers loved their husbands so fiercely is another thing you share."

Caroline's mouth opened but she didn't have a reply to make. Their mothers' marriages hadn't entered the conversation at all. And Caroline didn't intend to discuss her feelings on the topic with Lady Worth.

"I got the impression that your daughter didn't enjoy her Season, and that has left a bad feeling about it with Lady Catherine."

"Really?" Lady Worth questioned. "I would have thought she would have nothing but good things to say since it was how she met my son-in-law." Lady Worth's face grew troubled. "Do you think Catherine will have a hard time in Town?"

Caroline reached out and squeezed Lady Worth's hand. "You did the right thing having her join your party this week. It will help her feel more comfortable in company and perhaps the other young ladies' excitement will rub off. Miss Nesbitt in particular is most enthused about the Season."

"But not you?"

Caroline wished to avoid Lady Worth's searching gaze but knew her smile would be weak. "I too have mixed feelings on the topic."

"Well, my dear, I know your father isn't gentry, but your mother loved him fiercely and it never seemed to me that she regretted her decision. It was a thing to behold how happy she was. Now I wouldn't necessarily recommend her course of action, but I can see your father was right for ensuring you entered Society." There was a brief pause while Caroline just stared at her hostess, at a loss for words. Lady Worth nodded. "Now you run along and enjoy your shopping."

Obediently Caroline turned, in a bit of a daze, and followed some of the other women from the inn.

Chapter Fourteen

Gilbert didn't know what to make of Caroline. She had marched away from his carriage as though on a mission. He had been certain she was going to tell all and sundry what they had been talking about and Gil had wracked his brain trying to come up with plausible explanations he could claim that would mitigate the situation without damaging her. Claiming she was a candidate for Bedlam had crossed his mind, but that would have ruined her for sure.

He might not have been too far off the mark, though, he thought with amusement as he continued to watch her from the corner of his eye, even as he tried to appear normal and circulate the room a little bit. He finally found himself in conversation with Mr. Smith himself for the first time that day.

"Did my daughter behave herself on the drive here?" the older man asked with laughter ringing in his voice that indicated he was jesting. Gilbert couldn't imagine why he would ask such a question.

"In what way would you think she might possibly misbehave in a moving carriage?"

Mr. Smith laughed a little louder than Gil thought was warranted. "There are any manner of ways, my boy, but I was thinking she might have tried to tell you how to drive. My daughter has an unfortunate tendency to be managing, particularly when she is nervous."

Gilbert frowned slightly. "And driving with me would be likely to make her nervous?"

"I would have expected so. Did she not seem nervous to you?"

Gilbert thought back over their conversation. He hadn't noticed any nerves at the time, but it was possible, in hindsight, to see that it might have been the case.

"Interesting insight, Mr. Smith. But no, she did not try to tell me how to drive. Perhaps she has reserved that for the drive back."

Mr. Smith laughed again. "I like you," he commented with approval, making heat prickle up the back of Gilbert's neck. He was investigating the man. It didn't seem right that the man would take a liking to him. If he were to know the truth he wouldn't be quite so amiable, Gil was sure.

He suddenly remembered Caroline's outrageous suggestion that he include Mr. Smith in the investigation. Gil obviously couldn't do so overtly, but perhaps he could feel him out a little bit.

"Do you ever encounter those who want things to remain the same and resist your efforts to bring the advancements into popularity?"

Mr. Smith stared at him for a second before shaking his head sadly. "All the time. It's most vexing. One would think they would be happy to see improvements."

"Not everyone agrees that change is an improvement."

Mr. Smith's frown was fierce. "Are you one of them, Mr. Northcott? It's usually the landowners who are the most resistant. I didn't think you were one of them, but

I suppose your father would be so you could be in the same line of thought as him."

Gil grinned. "No, I'm neither a landowner nor a resister," he countered. "But I do understand some of the resistance. On the other hand, I don't think resistance is of any use. I understand why some might not like it, but it cannot be prevented. I think it's quite inevitable, to be honest. And those who are trying to stop it are fighting a losing battle."

"And yet they continue to try," Mr Smith added mournfully before visibly brightening. "You could be quite helpful to me, my boy. Do you have gainful employment?"

Gilbert was certainly not expecting that response and hesitated in how to answer. "What did you have in mind?" he asked in order to buy some time. It wouldn't hurt to hear what the older man had to say. But Gilbert didn't have a good feeling about that conversation. He was beginning to suspect that Caroline was right. Her father was either an exceptionally good actor or he wasn't involved in the plot Gilbert had been sent to investigate. He was also reasonably convinced that Caroline was equally innocent.

But since there was irrefutable evidence that there was indeed a plot afoot, perhaps the businessman could help as his daughter had suggested. Gilbert would cover all his bases and find out.

"With your connections, we could ensure that the train lines get through. Especially in your father's part of the country, there is no one willing to allow it to pass by their lands. If we could educate the people that sheep and cows are just fine with the low noise that the passing trains make, we could surely make progress."

"How do you know for certain that the animals are fine with it?"

Mr. Smith chuckled. "Well, I'd like to tell you I asked them, but that would get me locked up in a hospital for certain, wouldn't it?" He shook his head and laughed again before continuing, "I've had trains passing through my lands for an age and the birthrates and health of my animals haven't changed. I'm not a biologist by any means, but I'd take that as proof."

Gilbert nodded. He was far from an expert, but he also wasn't terribly concerned about that, either. It wasn't as though the trains would be passing by all day long and most fields were large enough the animals could get away from the tracks if the noise bothered them overly.

"I could speak with my father," Gilbert stated. It was an easy enough promise as he had already had discussions with the earl about allowing tracks to go through parts of their lands. It was the way of the future, and it would surely benefit them in many ways between getting their materials faster and allowing their staff members to visit family more conveniently. Gilbert couldn't really see the downside his father was so determined to look upon.

"Who do you think is the main culprit in stirring up resistance to the tracks, Mr. Smith?" Gilbert finally thought it was safe to ask his question without causing the man suspicion.

"I'm not really comfortable answering that in noble company, Mr. Northcott," the older man finally replied after staring at him for a long moment that had made Gilbert squirm.

Gil's eyebrows rose. "I'm not nobility," he answered.

"Maybe not, but your father and brother certainly are. You're certainly gentry, so near enough. And there are others in this very room." He looked around as though to ascertain that no one was listening to them. Even though Gilbert didn't think anyone could hear

162

them, Mr. Smith lowered his voice even more. "If you really want to know my thoughts on the subject, you can speak to me tomorrow. I've heard we're to be playing at archery. We'll be outdoors and can stand far enough away from anyone else to be able to speak freely."

Gilbert wasn't convinced of the wisdom of engaging the successful businessman in such a discussion, but there was nothing he could do about it now. He wasn't really committed. As the other man said, Gil would have to approach him for the information if he wanted it.

But Gilbert knew that if he truly wanted to be thorough in his investigation, now that he had started down the path of questioning Mr. Smith, he would have to see it through. He would just have to make sure he did it in such a way as to keep the man ignorant of the fact that he was, in fact, investigating the matter. Gil sighed. He was sufficiently experienced in sounding like an empty-headed gadabout as Caroline had described him, he should be able to ask a few questions without revealing what he knew. But he still needed to ensure the young woman didn't tell her father what she knew.

Gil was relieved to see that Lady Worth intended for the arrangements to remain the same for the drive back to Chester Hill after everyone had spent time in the shops of the village. He was surprised to note that his passenger had very few parcels when he handed her up into his carriage.

"None of the items were fine enough for your taste?" he asked, feeling a little snide.

She frowned at him and then laughed a little even as an uneasy expression crossed her face at the way his hands lingered on her waist.

"Everything was actually quite lovely. I've arranged for a few things to be sent home by messenger. I wasn't sure if there would be room in my carriage for some of things I wanted."

Gilbert wanted to kick himself for his foolishness. The woman didn't owe him a single explanation. Nor was there a reason for him to accuse her of – what exactly *had* he been trying to accuse her of? He couldn't even tell. The entire situation was turning his mind.

They drove in silence for a few minutes while she kept her face averted, seemingly watching the passing scenery, but Gilbert could almost hear the weight of her thoughts, like the slow turning of a heavy train.

"I suppose you want me to keep it a secret that you're some sort of agent," she finally said to him, careful to keep her voice to a volume that he could just hear over the clop of the horses' hooves.

"Yes, it is a matter of national importance and as such needs to remain secret." Gilbert grimaced over how pompous that made him sound. She seemed to ignore that and simply nodded.

"I saw you speaking with my father. Did you take my suggestion and ask him?"

"In a manner of speaking. I didn't actually mean to do so. But it sort of came up." He paused and sighed. "It's possible you're right. He has information that can help me whether he's involved or not."

"You aren't convinced, then, of his innocence?"

Gilbert shrugged. "I'm not convinced of anyone's innocence," he answered with an attempt at a light laugh. "But in this particular case, no, I'll say, not yet."

The woman nodded, looking quite serious and terribly determined. "Then how can I help you? This needs to be cleared up as quickly as possible or it could ruin me and adversely affect him." She paused for a moment before adding, "To be perfectly honest, I don't much care about my social standing but I know it would break my father's heart and I will not allow you to do that. I still don't know what you think you could find out here at a house party, but I will tell you whatever I might possibly know and try to find out what I can from anyone else present as discretely as possible." She paused again, staring at the flickering ears of the horses while a small smile lifted the corners of her lips. "The animals would be able to tell you if only they could."

Gilbert stared at her. What a strange thing to say. But he supposed she wasn't wrong. Horses were far more intuitive than many expected. Besides the conversations they no doubt overheard. He smiled at the thought. Too bad he couldn't question the horses.

"I appreciate your offer of help, Miss Smith," he finally said. "And your promise of discretion. It's in everyone's best interests if it remains between us. So continued discretion will be key. Do you think you are capable of questioning others without it seeming strange?"

The young woman shrugged. "I have been a wallflower throughout the Season. I think people might expect strange from me." Her smile was so sunny that it somehow made Gilbert's chest ache. He couldn't believe she had restored herself to her usual equilibrium. She shrugged again as though they were not discussing such an important matter. "I would think my asking about industrial matters might not be so very strange for people, considering my father's affairs. Surely his daughter would be expected to take at least a slight interest. Lady St. John assured me that I was to abstain from all conversations about business in order to maintain my distance from his filthy funds, but I think at a house party those sorts of strictures might understandably loosen somewhat."

Gilbert laughed. "Did she actually call them filthy funds?"

Caroline laughed, too. "No, that is my term. I like the alliteration. And it is fitting since that seems to be how the *ton* views it. It is the strangest thing, is it not? If he was a duke who had inherited his fortune, those very same amounts would be spoken of with reverence but because he earned it, somehow it is unacceptable." She turned and met his gaze. "What a contrary lot you nobles are."

Gilbert couldn't argue with her on that. He turned the subject. "I noticed you spent quite a bit of time with our hostess' granddaughter at luncheon. She has struck me as being so very quiet. How did you manage to get her to open up to you?"

Caroline lifted a shoulder in a rather self-deprecating gesture as a mixture of feelings tripped across her features. He would have missed it if he hadn't been watching her so carefully despite his need to watch the road and guide his horses. It was endearing. As though she were pleased by his noticing. Gilbert pushed the thought away. The chit couldn't get ideas in her head about his interest. She was a means to an end. Perhaps if he told himself often enough he would start to believe it.

"She is quite a shy young lady but very pleasant. I didn't realize someone born into such a position could be so nervous about it. I hope I was able to allay some of her fears. Her grandmother was right to have her come to the house party and get a bit of practice before braving the full force of Society." She paused for a moment with a slight frown on her face. "Have you ever met the lady's parents? It seems her mother had a deeply held fear of Society that she has passed on to her daughter."

"I've met his lordship but, while I never really noticed it, you're right, his wife never came to Town."

Caroline nodded. "So the poor young woman never really prepared for a Season in the traditional sense of anticipating it with delight. She has been given the proper instructions, of course, and knows how to dance and comport herself, but the only practice she has ever had has been within her family." She turned her penetrating gaze away from watching the road and skewered him with it. "You will have to be sure to dance with her whenever Lady Worth has dancing. You are very skilled and shall be most excellent practice for her."

Gilbert laughed. "You have suddenly become quite the dictator."

He watched as pink crept up from her neck but she didn't cower despite her discomfort. Instead she tried to shrug it off. "Not a dictator. But she has had a rough go of it. All she needs is a little bit of assistance."

"Seems to me your stories are similar."

"Not terribly so," Caroline countered with a light laugh. "We're just both motherless."

"And your situations with your mothers makes Society a bit of a trial for you. The circumstances might be different but the result is much the same."

Her eyes widened as though she hadn't thought of that, and Gilbert felt his chest tighten once more. She was a delightful girl. But he wasn't in the market, he reminded himself.

"How do you think to proceed in helping me with my investigation?" He turned the subject again to remind them both of the reason for their association.

"For one thing, I have mentally assembled a list of all I can think of who might be capable of stirring up trouble for the train lines. Whenever you're ready I can share those names with you. Also, I will be able to bring up conversations about train travel and such when you will be nearby to watch and listen for people's reactions. This way, it isn't you bringing it up, which might appear strange to some, but I'm assuming you have experience in watching for people's reactions. And it shan't be strange for me as an industrialist's daughter to be excited about these newfangled things."

Gilbert laughed. It was a good plan. And should be quite easily accomplished.

Chapter Fifteen

C aroline tried not to allow her heart to squeeze at the sound of his rich laughter. Mr. Northcott was not for her. Papa might be willing to overlook his lack of title in order to be so closely connected with the Earl of Everleigh, but Caro was certain that, despite her father's loyalty to their King and country, he would not wish to see her embroiled in an agent's life. Even if the thought filled her with excitement. What a fulfilling life that would be! But the strange flutters she experienced whenever she was in Gilbert's company assured Caroline he was not for her. She had promised herself she would not so disrupt her life and independence by succumbing to a love match and Lady Worth's words were not enough to make her go back on her vow.

She turned her face to watch the scenery pass by once more. No, Gilbert's association with her was just a means to an end for both of them. She needed to protect her father and her reputation. He had an investigation to get to the bottom of. It was temporary. They were not friends. She only hoped she could keep her heart from believing otherwise.

"I should have thought to involve you from the start, especially when you first questioned me about what I was up to. I'd likely be much further along."

Caroline smiled. "Quite likely," she agreed with a shrug. "But men usually have to learn the hard way rather than the easy way."

She was surprised when he didn't appear in the least disturbed by her words. "You are probably more correct than even you might realize."

They rode in companionable silence for a while before he tried to strike up a conversation again.

"What did you think of the village?"

"It was charming. Every business seemed happy for the patronage. It always makes me uncomfortable when I enter a shop, and it feels like I'm disturbing them rather than bringing them business."

"Does that happen to you?" Gilbert sounded incredulous. "I suppose I don't actually do much of my own shopping so I haven't experienced this."

Caroline nodded. "I suppose it must be a challenging balance to find if you have to produce the items you are trying to sell. When they find the time for everything, I can't even begin to imagine."

"You seem to have an empathetic heart, Miss Smith."

Caroline wasn't sure if he was complimenting her or not, so she merely nodded. There was no arguing with that. Her imagination often allowed her to see where people's troubles lie. It was both a blessing and a curse.

"What about you, Mr. Northcott? Did you enjoy the time we spent in the village?"

Gilbert frowned a little as though he were undecided. "It felt like a waste of my time since I couldn't very well search anyone's room or further my investigation."

170

Caroline turned a wide eyed stare upon him. "Have you been searching people's rooms? How very irregular."

Gilbert laughed. "I haven't been successful with it yet. I was hoping to enlist your help with that effort."

Heat infused Caroline at the thought. She was sure to create a scandal. It would deeply embarrass her father. And Lady St. John. Caroline swallowed. She had barely given the older woman a thought all day. She was a dreadful protégé. Her heart sank with the realization.

"I cannot fathom how you think we could do such a thing without getting caught."

"We will just have to make sure we don't get caught." The man said it as though it was the simplest thing in the world.

"Do you not feel as though you are violating some sort of unspoken agreement? As in, do the other guests not have a reasonable expectation of privacy? And doesn't Lady Worth deserve our respect in not violating her guests' privacy in such an offensive manner?"

She watched as his jaw clenched. "This isn't some simple little matter, Miss Smith. Lives could be at stake. If the plot goes through, there could be terrible accidents that could ruin people's lives or even end them. What is a little privacy when that is at stake?"

Caroline swallowed the lump forming in her throat. She wished she had never noticed the man's over interest in her father. This venture was not going to lead to anything good. She shook her head. That was a cowardly thought. If she hadn't noticed and hadn't involved herself, the man was heading toward ruining her father. By involving herself, she could protect her father and maybe even herself. But it violated every one of her personal sensitivities.

171

"How do you propose we search?" She could hear how shaky her voice sounded and hated her cowardice, but she was new to the world of spying. He would have to put up with her bout of nerves.

"There's my girl. I knew you could buck up."

She didn't want to feel bolstered by his words but felt herself do so anyway. She waited to see if he would actually answer her question.

"We will first have to ascertain if there is some sort of schedule of the servants' movements. It is in everyone's best interests if we do not get caught, as you said. So if we can figure out when the servants straighten the rooms, we will have the best chance of being able to look around without anyone being the wiser."

Caroline nodded. It still left so much to chance, but she couldn't think of a better idea. All of this was starting to make her stomach hurt, but she didn't see that she had another choice. It would be better to involve herself than to leave it all to chance. And while she was realizing that this man hid so much of himself and was actually much more intelligent and even kinder than he let on, she didn't know him well enough to trust him with her future. She needed to see this through.

She couldn't tell her father even if she wanted to, anyway. He was too distracted by his flirtation with Lady Fanny. Caroline couldn't understand what the attraction could possibly be. She ought to pursue the subject further with her father, but he hadn't really appreciated it when she had tried to bring it up before. What a conundrum. This house party was turning out to be the best of times and the worst of times all rolled into one experience.

"If it appears that we have taken an interest in one another, it might make it less suspicious if we are seen to be spending time together." Gilbert's voice was low, and Caroline had to take a second to discern his meaning.

"If we are spending time together, won't people just assume that we have taken an interest in one another? That seems to be the automatic response, isn't it?" Caroline was confused. What was he trying to say without saying it?

The man grew even more uncomfortable under her gaze.

"Are you trying to make sure I don't get the wrong idea about the time we're about to spend together?" she asked with a nervous laugh.

He couldn't meet her gaze, confirming her words. Caroline sighed. She had thought she hadn't allowed herself to get the wrong idea already, but the hurt she was feeling in that moment would seem to belie her efforts.

"Well, thank you for the warning. I will do my utmost not to find you excessively attractive." She hoped her dry tone allowed him to think she didn't. How mortifying that would be.

He suddenly laughed. "You are the most amusing creature I've ever met, Miss Smith."

"Why thank you, kind sir. This is exactly what every young woman wants to hear."

Gilbert laughed again. "My apologies, my wits have gone begging today, it would seem. I certainly meant you no insult. I've just never encountered a woman such as you."

Caroline shrugged, growing uncomfortable. "I'm no different than most, really, Mr. Northcott. Most people are very similar under all the trappings."

"Not in my experience," he insisted.

"Well then your experience must not be very broad," she returned promptly and with a tart little bite in her tone, causing him to chuckle anew but not comment further.

"Do promise you'll save me a dance if there is to be dancing this evening."

"Perhaps. But I'm not certain I wish everyone to think we're so very interested in one another just yet."

Gilbert actually blushed. Caroline could have crowed with her triumph for such a feat. She had wanted to offset him slightly for having made her so uncomfortable. She felt in this case turnabout was fair play. Besides, he was being ridiculous to even ask. As if she would refuse his hand in a dance. And it was unlikely there would be so many clamouring for her hand that he wouldn't be able to claim her if he so wished.

Soft hearted as she was, she couldn't leave it there, though. She reached over and patted his arm. "Of course I'll dance with you if you ask me. There's just no need to make a reservation."

Caroline quickly withdrew her hand. She had meant to offer him comfort, which had probably been presumptuous on her part, but touching him never failed to result in exactly the sort of feelings she wanted to quash entirely.

Chapter Sixteen

Mortification flooded Gilbert. The girl was actually trying to offer him comfort as though she might have wounded him with her teasing. What a strange girl. He couldn't even look at her at this point. He needed to keep any feelings out of this situation. Either positive or negative, he reminded himself. He was supposed to be a version of neutral even though he had been sent here with a certain premise. If the facts led him in a different direction, he needed to follow them.

He couldn't allow his respect for the girl to cloud his judgment about her father. It had just been a matter of days earlier when he had actually been thinking that the girl could be part of the problem. And now here he was wishing he could make it all better for her. If he wasn't careful he was going to wind up a candidate for Bedlam.

It was a relief when they arrived back at Chester Hill.

The days soon began to blur together.

The day for the archery activities came and went. It hadn't been the day after the visit to the village as Mr. Smith had thought, due to a couple days of rain that kept them mostly confined to indoor activities. But finally, the day dawned bright and clear and Lady Worth declared it the perfect day to play with bows and arrows. Gilbert thought it would be a recipe for disaster, but he was really looking forward to getting out of the house. He had already gotten up early and gone for a bruising gallop on his favorite horse in order to blow out some of the cobwebs from his mind.

He had managed to exchange coded messages with the Home Office which had set his mind at ease somewhat. His investigation was not moving forward, and he was beginning to fear failure. It was not a feeling he was familiar with. But at least other agents were progressing. And really, if Mr. Smith was truly innocent, then he supposed establishing that couldn't really be considered a failure.

From what Lord Chamberlain or one of his clerks had written, nothing had been found during any of the searches at Smith's properties, so really, that only went to show that either he was far wilier than any of them suspected or he had no involvement in the plot against the rail advancements. But the threats remained in place. The Home Office was convinced there was an active plot, and they expected Gilbert to continue his investigation at Chester Hill.

Miss Smith had done her best to help him. She had given him a list of anyone she could think of who might have enough knowledge of the railroads or the train technology to be a threat to them. She had also been initiating conversations about technology as often as she could manage without drawing undue attention. Gilbert had started to notice that it hadn't escaped her chaperone's notice, though. The older woman's face was a study in puzzlement whenever Caroline would start talking about railroads or steam engines. It would be highly diverting if the matter at hand were not so terribly serious.

"Have you been for a train ride yet, Lord Thornwood?" She asked it with such a sweet, inquisitive smile that no one could possibly know she had calculated who would be best to ask. They had actually discussed it in great detail. Gilbert was impressed with her understanding of the way the human mind thinks.

"It's a bit of a risk. Since Lord Thornwood is the highest level of Society present other than the Worths, if he scoffs at the idea, no one else will want to express any interest. But if he is either neutral or positive, we have a better chance of finding out what the others think."

"I've known Thorn for years. He isn't likely to be a scoffer."

Gilbert held his breath as he awaited his friend's response, hoping he wasn't about to be proven a liar.

"I haven't yet had the chance to take a ride, Miss Smith. But I did visit the engine manufacturer."

"Oh, how delightful. Were you fascinated?"

Gilbert's eyebrow rose. The woman might be playing it a bit too brown. She was rarely this animated about anything. Of course, as she had pointed out, this topic was one she was actually truly interested in. Evidently that made a difference. Even if no one else was fascinated by the engines, they couldn't help being fascinated by her.

Thorn's smile reflected that truth, and Gilbert had to exert effort not to react visibly.

"I'm not certain I would deem it fascination, but it was definitely an interesting visit." The viscount's response wasn't enthusiastic, but he didn't condemn her interest.

"Are you an investor in the venture, my lord?"

She asked the question with wide, eager eyes as though anxious or excited to hear his answer. But Gilbert was certain it was merely a ploy. If he were an investor it would go a ways toward proving he couldn't be involved, in Caroline's estimation. Of course, if he accepted that argument, then he would have to accept that her father wasn't involved either. But he was still interested to hear what Thorn would answer.

"I do have an interest in them, yes. I shouldn't be so surprised to see you having knowledge of the subject, I suppose. I have to admit, it wasn't with your father that I invested."

Caroline's laugh was light when she replied. "That's quite all right, my lord. I don't think it would be possible to admit everyone who wished to invest in my father's ventures. But there are plenty of other companies who are nearly as reputable." She paused and smiled around at the others who were listening to their conversation. "Now tell me, why did you not take a ride? You surely were not afraid, were you?"

Gilbert couldn't help the burst of laughter that escaped him at her question. The chit was actually flirting with his friend right under his nose. Not that he wished her to be flirting with he himself, Gilbert reminded himself once more. But still. A little decorum would be appreciated.

But it seemed like it had been the exact right thing to say as everyone else had laughed as well and then a lively discussion had ensued about the benefits that were sure to come with the ability to travel more swiftly than by carriage.

"But what will become of all the horses?" Miss Nesbitt had asked, bringing another round of good natured laughter.

Caroline had patted her hand. "No need to worry. It will be quite some time before everyone accepts the new things. I am certain horses will be around for a good long time yet."

Everyone had laughed a little bit more and then it had been easy enough to gently question each of the gentlemen present about their possible involvement with the railroads. Most had a modicum of knowledge on the subject with very little interest in pursuing more, much to Miss Smith's hastily suppressed disgust. Gilbert was certain no one other than he had noticed her reaction, but he could tell she was disappointed that the gentlemen were so uninterested. He didn't want to think too deeply about why that would bother her. But he supposed they were all still to be considered potential marriage mates for her. It was clear Caroline was interested in matters of industry. It would no doubt be a challenge for her to marry someone who had no interest, or worse, thought it beneath them.

A little bit of Gilbert's guilt over involving her dissipated in that moment. It was good for her to see which gentleman might share her interests. Even if she was disappointed. It was far better to be disappointed now than later.

He was impressed with her ability to keep smiling through it all. Her smile only faltered when Miss Brigham asked an ill-mannered question about finances.

"Surely there's no money to be made in train travel, though, is there?" There had been something in Lady Fanny's niece's voice that had both Gilbert and seemingly Caroline on alert.

"Why would you say that? I would recommend it as a sound investment," Caroline had finally replied when no one else seemed forthcoming with a comment.

Miss Brigham didn't appear to have a ready response so the conversation carried on, but it continued to scratch at the back of Gilbert's mind in the following days.

And then the archery day was upon them.

There was an air of excitement shimmering over the assembled gentry. Not surprising considering they had been cooped up indoors for two days straight due to constant drizzle. But the conversation over breakfast was louder than usual and more were assembled as well. Gilbert noted that most of the women had developed the custom of having their breakfast served to them in their rooms rather than descending to the breakfast room. But not that day. The table was full and the conversation flowing.

"Have you ever shot an arrow before?"

"Isn't the sunshine lovely?"

"I'm an excellent shot."

"Doesn't it take a great deal of strength?"

It seemed to Gilbert that no one was really listening to anyone else. Except Caroline, of course. He could see that her eyes were swiveling from face to face while her face held a delighted smile. Finally she answered the question that seemed to most need an answer. She turned to Lady Catherine.

"Not a great deal of strength, no, but you will probably find your arm a little sore later if you manage to do well. It will probably be a much different movement than you're used to if you've never tried it before. But as a woman who loves to ride, you should actually be quite fine at it."

"Do you think so?" The young woman seemed to have remarkably poor confidence in herself for someone so well-born. Gilbert watched as Caroline offered her reassurance.

"Absolutely," she answered firmly. "Riding takes more strength than you might realize, even if you have never saddled a horse for yourself before. You shall see. It will be great fun."

Gilbert could see that the young ladies didn't look completely convinced but they were willing to be enthusiastic, nonetheless.

"Have no fear, my lady, I'll be happy to demonstrate for you."

It was all Gilbert could do not to roll his eyes at Mr. Browne but then all the young women were clamouring for promises of demonstrations and the gentlemen were exclaiming over their own prowess. Caroline's gaze met his and the laughter dancing therein did strange things to Gilbert's equilibrium. She was a dangerous woman.

He was still reasonably confident that she was innocent of espionage, but her intelligence and understanding of people made her a worthy, if unwanted, partner and would make her a formidable agent if he were to tell the Office about her abilities. Gilbert wasn't sure if he ought to admit to the Home Office that he had needed to rely upon an assistant.

But she had certainly been of help.

And now the archery. It was, as Mr. Smith had said, an excellent opportunity to be able to speak without anyone paying much attention.

After he had taken a few shots, Gil passed his bow off to someone else and tried to appear as though he were merely wandering away. He approached Mr. Smith as casually as he could manage even though he was now very anxious to hear the man's thoughts. He was no further ahead in his investigation than he had been when he had first arrived at Chester Hill. If anything, it could be argued that he was further behind as now more than a week had passed and he could neither prove Mr. Smith's guilt nor his innocence. Again he was left to wonder how it had been expected that he would be able to do either at a house party.

Aside from talking to the man directly, the only thing that was left was searching everyone's rooms more thoroughly than he had been able to do the first time. Gilbert was well aware that Caroline didn't want to be involved with that, but he wasn't going to be able to let her off without helping. It would be better for both of them if he were to have her help.

"Your aim was quite true, Northcott," Roger Smith complimented as Gilbert approached him.

"Thank you." What else was he supposed to say? He had nearly hit the center of the target Lady Worth had arranged at the end of the lawn.

"Your daughter seems quite well informed about your various investments, Mr. Smith, and very enthusiastic in her support."

The expression that crossed the older man's face was a mixture of pride and disappointment. "Is the girl talking too much? I've warned her not to demonstrate her interest so much. In fact, I've tried to tell her she shouldn't be interested at all, but she won't have it."

"Why would you wish her to not be interested in your affairs?"

"You lot don't appreciate that sort of thing in your womenfolk," the man near sputtered in his conflicted feelings, making Gilbert smile.

Gil shrugged. "Many don't, you're right, but still, it seems only natural that a daughter would take an interest in what her father is involved in. Especially since you are each all the other has." He paused and watched the man's face carefully as he asked his next question. "Are you afraid it's unsafe for her?"

"Unsafe? Why would it be unsafe? I don't invest in anything I think might be harmful to anyone, especially not my Caroline." The man had been on the defensive at first, but then his face softened. "Are you still thinking about who might be opposed to advancements? You are even more strange than the marquis," he observed with a shake of his head, making Gilbert's smile widen. Mr. Smith stepped closer and lowered his voice but seemed to be trying to look innocent or nonchalant even as he leaned in to share secrets. "It's the Royal Dukes."

"Excuse me?"

"You wanted to know who I thought would be making the most effort to resist change. It's the Royal Dukes who least want anything to change. They quite like their comfortable positions, and the only time they can bestir themselves is to make trouble for His Highness. They don't want change unless it's to their benefit. They don't see railroads as something that could benefit them, so they're stirring up trouble."

Gilbert agreed with Mr. Smith's assessment, but that still didn't relieve the older man of involvement in said trouble nor explain his association with Duncan and his comrades.

"Have you ever met any of them?"

"Royalty isn't likely to be lowering themselves to spending time with the likes me now, are they?"

Gilbert lifted a shoulder in a little shrug. "If you had something they wanted, they would probably be willing."

Roger laughed as though Gilbert had been jesting but then his shrewd eyes narrowed. "You are a strange one, Mr. Northcott." With a shake of his head he started to walk away. Before Gilbert could reclaim his attention, he heard his name being called.

"It's your turn again, Northcott."

He bit back the oath he wished to utter and tried to keep a pleasant expression as he returned to the activities of the day.

Noise and action and conversation flowed around them all day, and the time flew by. Just as they were about to return to their chambers to change for supper, Gilbert was finally able to speak quietly with Caroline for the briefest moment.

"There's no other way around it. We'll have to search the rooms."

She looked as though he had struck her, and for the briefest moment he thought she was going to be ill right in front of him before she blinked her reaction away. With a slight nod but no words she acknowledged that she had heard him and then walked away.

Chapter Seventeen

C aroline knew she could never send the letter, but she was writing it anyway.

Dear Daisy:

I wish you were here. I was having a good time even without you, at first. But then it all changed. Mr. Northcott is an agent of some sort. For the King. And they suspect my father of being involved in some plot against the railroads. He won't tell me anything else. And the only way I can save my father and my own reputation is if I help him with the investigation.

Caroline glanced around the room where there were several ladies leaning over piles of paper. Even though no one was paying attention to her, she knew she needed to be extra careful as she wrote. But it was the only way she could work through her feelings. While she had always kept her thoughts to herself and had never really felt the need to confide in anyone, this problem felt too big, and there was no one she could talk to. Daisy had been her favorite person she had yet met this Season. At least her favorite of the other young ladies seeking a mate. And while Caroline would never actually send this letter, somehow it was a comfort to feel as though she were pouring out her heart to someone she could trust. Even if she couldn't actually do it for real.

I'm not sure if I'm actually going to manage to save my reputation. Gilbert wants to search some of the other guests' rooms, of all the daft ideas. And he needs me to help him do it. Or at least to stand as a lookout while he does it. If we were to be caught, I'll be ruined for certain. But if it gets out that my father is suspected of such a heinous crime I'll be ruined anyway, so how can I not involve myself?

With a sigh, Caroline looked away from her paper once more before she carried on, hoping that her inner turmoil wasn't written plainly all over her face.

Even worse than all of this, though, my dear Daisy, is that I had actually thought for a brief moment that he might be trying to court me. Is that not the most ridiculous thing you've ever heard? As if a son of the Earl of Everleigh would court one such as me unless his pockets were to let. Even though he's a younger son, he doesn't seem like he's about to go begging. But there you have it. I am completely foolish. When he was spending time with me and watching my father, I thought he might have taken an interest in us or me to be more specific. It turns out, of course, that he had, just not one of the romantic sort. And I hate to admit it, but my heart hurt just a little bit. Which is exactly what I don't want, so I suppose it's just as well that I'm courting scandal as I do not want to be courting someone who will affect my heart.

So now I must decide if I can tolerate Lord Powell for the rest of my born days. My father is less enthusiastic than he was at first about that particular gentleman. But what else am I to do? Leave Chester Hill without a match? Go back to Town and hope someone else comes up to scratch?

You haven't sent any great detail about the goings on in Town. Have you found a match yet yourself? I know you were hoping for it to happen sooner rather than later for yourself. I cannot blame you. I am left with weighing between returning to Town or accepting Lord Powell, and I cannot decide which is the worse option. I would almost like to come back to Town if you will be there to enjoy the rest of the Season with.

Caroline crumpled her paper up into a tight ball before realizing that wasn't good enough. She could never take a chance of it getting into anyone's hands. Glancing around the room to ensure no one was paying her any heed, Caroline stood up and quietly left the room. She would rip up the paper and burn the pieces. It had been a relief to express her feelings, but it would be a disaster if her thoughts were to fall into someone else's hands. It had actually been quite foolish to relieve herself in such a way.

It was a challenge not to allow her heart to get involved with Gilbert Northcott as they spent more time together. And now he was going to ruin her. Should she confide in Lady St. John? But what good would that do? There was every chance the older woman would overreact and do her own part in ruining Caroline, either in an effort to help or as a way to protect her own daughter.

Caroline glanced at herself in the mirror and frowned at the wide-eyed reflection she saw there. Squaring her shoulders, she glared at herself. She would just have to make sure they weren't caught and she wasn't ruined.

A tall order but surely she could do it.

She wasn't even certain when Gilbert thought they'd be able to make the attempt to search. On the one hand, the best time would be when everyone had free time to do as they wished. It would be the least likely that anyone would think either of them were missing. But it was also the time that they would be the least able to guarantee where anyone else was. So it was the best time and the worst time.

Caroline stuck her head out of her room and looked both ways, straining to hear if there was any activity. Today was not the day they had agreed to the search, but Caroline thought she would do a little surveillance in an effort to make herself more comfortable with the ordeal to come.

It didn't help. The butterflies fluttering in her midsection didn't subside until she was well away from the guest quarters. Which was beyond foolish. She had every right to be near her own bedchamber. No one would even question it, she assured herself. But guilt sat heavy upon her. And it was only going to get worse.

They had agreed to meet midmorning the next day and Caroline lived through a blur until then.

Everything felt foggy and she regretted that as there were important things taking place around her and she couldn't focus enough to take it in.

Lady Fanny was still pursuing her father. Caroline was only partially comforted by the fact that it didn't appear as though Mr. Smith was returning the noblewoman's affections any longer.

The only bright spot that penetrated the fog surrounding her was the fact that Lord Powell's affections seemed to have become divided. Caroline had to smile as he tried to spread himself between several of the young ladies that evening.

The surrounding gentry had been invited for dancing, and the ballroom was almost as full as one in London might be. Caroline was certain Lady Worth would be happy with the success of her entertainment, but she herself was no longer enjoying herself. In an effort to calm her thoughts, Caroline imagined herself at home in Somerset with her lifelong servants and neighbours. The thoughts did comfort her briefly, but then her eyes popped open and sought out Gilbert Northcott.

He came to claim her for a dance.

"Is someone searching my home right now?" She asked it as quietly as she could, but even she could hear the accusation in her tone. And she watched as heat rose on his neck, indicating she was right. Nausea threatened for a brief moment but she managed to swallow it down, keep smiling, and not even miss a single step of the dance. The fog actually helped in that moment.

Her ruination might be a foregone conclusion after all, she realized with a sense of despair.

"That makes far more sense than searching here. Are you also searching the marquis' other properties?"

"Why would you think that?"

"Because it's not only the commoners who can perform criminal acts." Her tone had been dry and accusatory. "My apologies. My feelings are a bit of a jumble."

His features had softened and for the briefest moment Caroline wanted to throw herself into his arms to seek comfort. Well, she was already in his arms, in the dance, so she supposed it was a misguided desire to throw herself deeper into his arms. She stifled the urge.

"I am well aware that criminals are not confined to class. But why would you suspect Lord Worth?"

Caroline frowned at him, surprised at his question. "He is the only one who really knows anything or has taken any sort of interest in the railroads, didn't you notice? Whenever it was brought up, he was the only one who seemed intrigued."

"But surely you don't suspect him of wrong doing," Gilbert blustered.

Caroline shrugged. "I don't have an inborn tendency to think nobles are noble, I'm afraid. Quite the opposite, in fact. But no, I don't necessarily suspect him of anything. But if you're searching my father's house, it just seemed to my mind to stand to reason." Then, as he swirled her into the next turn of the dance, she smiled at him gently. "But what do I know?"

Chapter Eighteen

Gilbert watched the young woman in his arms and he ached. He literally ached. He knew full well Caroline was nearly at her wits' end and was doing her best to come to terms with what she faced. While he was very sure he needed her, he wished he didn't. But he was more than determined not to allow her to be ruined, which he knew was her biggest fear. Or rather more likely her second biggest. She was determined to protect her father first, herself second. And perhaps the railways third, he admitted with a soft smile.

"Has something happened?"

"Something like what?" She frowned ever so slightly even as she followed his lead perfectly.

"I don't know, but you seem more troubled than before."

For a moment she grinned widely at his question, as though delighted that he'd noticed. But then she lifted a shoulder in half a shrug. "I just envisioned doing it," she whispered the words so softly even he could barely hear her. "The searching," she elaborated in case he didn't understand. "And I haven't been completely right since." Her smile held a wealth of embarrassment. "Foolish of me, wasn't it?"

"Not necessarily. But you aren't going to back out on me are you?"

"Not unless you've suddenly seen reason and are going to drop the investigation into my father."

"It's nearly finished, I promise."

She actually rolled her eyes, and it was all Gilbert could do not to laugh out loud. She was a dear, amusing soul. If it wasn't a matter of such importance, he would do what he could to let her out of the investigation. Really, he had never had assistance before, so he shouldn't need it so much now. But he now felt certain he couldn't finish the investigation without her.

"At the very least, it will all soon be behind us," he reworded his statement.

"You are being daft," she said quite succinctly. "If we are caught, it will never be behind me. You, perhaps. Gentlemen so rarely face consequences. But not for me."

"Would you rather you weren't involved?"

Silence stretched between them. Gilbert thought it was obvious she would rather be anywhere but there. She surprised him when she finally spoke again.

"No. For many reasons, some of which I needn't explain to you. But no, I need to see for myself that my father is protected. I know he isn't guilty. You aren't so sure. Therefore, I need to remain involved if I cannot pass that burden to someone else. And really, there's no one I could pass it to except Papa, and I'm not sure that would be a solution."

Gilbert thought to change the subject as there was no getting around the truth of what she had said.

"Your father seems to be bearing up well under Lady Fanny's pursuit."

Caroline actually laughed a little over that. "Yes, well, I haven't yet met a man who would hate being pursued by a beautiful woman."

Gilbert frowned at her. "Do you really think she's beautiful? She gives me the impression that she's rather cold and cruel. That quite interferes with her beauty."

"That's true. But many men don't see that side of her. Most just see what they want to see, in all actuality."

Finally, to his relief and dismay, their dance came to an end and Caroline was claimed by one of the local gentlemen. Gilbert couldn't remember his name for a brief moment, but he couldn't help watching as they danced away from him. He turned his attention quite deliberately away from the dance floor and observed his fellow guests for a moment, wondering if any of them might actually be of concern to the Home Office.

Caroline had been quite correct. Lord Worth had been the only one who had shown any interest, besides Mr. Smith, in any of Caroline's efforts to discuss technology of any sort. All the younger men had been interested in sports and horses. Some of them had investments, of course, but none seemed to know very much about it. It had been amusing to watch Caroline try to keep her disappointment in check. She had expected the men to take more of an interest in her beloved industries.

Roger Smith was a fool in his determination to marry the girl into a noble's home. Not that she wouldn't be able to fit well into any situation she found herself. She'd make a remarkable duchess, in fact. Gil's respect for her continued to grow with the more time they spent together. But he was fairly certain a nobleman would happily spend her dowry and expect her to look pretty and be grateful. Gilbert didn't know anyone who would appreciate Caroline as she ought to be. He again thought that she would make an excellent agent. But he could never suggest that to her. Especially if she did end up wed to a nobleman.

While several of Gilbert's friends, and even his brothers, were involved with the Home Office, he knew none of them had involved their wives. In fact, the ones who had wed had all chosen to step back from their duties at the Office. Like his brother Lucian.

Gilbert knew he shouldn't have written to the viscount about his dilemma with Caroline, but he hadn't known what else to do. If the girl did get caught helping him in his investigation, he would have to do what he could to protect her from the scandal. As a single man, there wasn't much he could do to help her, but Viscount Adelaide and his new bride might actually be able to redirect any interest in her involvement. Lucian had assured him they would be at the ready and had even offered to enlist the earl if need be. Gil wasn't entirely certain how they would get Caroline through any possible scandal, but he thought they could perhaps force her relatives to help her brazen it out. He would rather not have to find out, of course, but having Lucian's promise of assistance had quelled some of his own concerns. It was the most in harmony he had felt with his brother in ages. It almost made him hope there *was* trouble of some sort just so he could solidify that bond with his brother.

But he couldn't wish that upon Caroline.

He did wish trouble upon her dance partner, though, he thought quite irrationally as he watched laughter light up her gaze as she turned it toward the young man's face over whatever inanities had just been uttered. She was remarkably adept socially for someone who had never spent much time amongst the *ton*.

Gilbert spent the rest of the evening alternating between dancing with the young ladies and observing his fellow guests. He couldn't decide if he was having more fun than he ever would have expected or if he was turning into a blathering idiot. He vacillated between the two extremes.

There were times when he thought *everyone* appeared suspicious. There was plenty of whispering behind fans and furtive glances. But that could just be flirting and courtship. This was either the most highly suspicious group of gentry that could have been assembled or it was all completely innocent. Two weeks was far too long to be immersed into an investigation like this. *What had his superiors been thinking?*

There was nothing for it but to search the rooms as he had said from the beginning. He really ought to have done it again sooner. Except that now, with the house party well underway, in fact, nearing its end, it was entirely possible that, if there were any guilty parties amongst them, they would have relaxed by now, expecting that they had escaped detection. So perhaps waiting this long was the best tactic he could have taken.

Except that it hadn't been a tactic. It had been him being lily-livered after having involved a civilian in his case. A gently bred female civilian. He was a fool.

But she was a gently bred female civilian with a backbone of steel and she was going to meet him in the hallway of the guest quarters in the middle of the next morning. In the meantime she danced, almost with abandon. Gilbert knew, though, that she was nearly drowning in her fears. She was remarkable. He didn't know many battle-hardened men who could demonstrate the courage she had shown.

Soon the evening passed and the guests were all drifting toward their chambers or calling for their carriages. The servants were performing their magic and erasing all trace of the festivities that had taken place, restoring order for the next day.

After the late night of dancing, it would be a slow morning the next day. It was the right time for the search. Unless anyone remained abed, of course.

Gilbert had enlisted the aid of his valet to ascertain from the servants if anyone did so. Especially the ladies. Not that he expected to find anything of note in any of the young women's chambers. But the married ladies were of particular note for him. Their husbands could be involved.

Caroline was nearly vibrating with nerves when she finally met him. She had come up with the plan to linger in the hallway to examine the artwork. It had been remarked upon on the first day, but she hadn't yet taken the opportunity to really examine each work.

"I only hope I don't become too absorbed in the art and forget about why we're here," she had whispered to him briefly with a wide smile that almost covered her nerves. Gilbert knew there was no chance of her forgetting.

"Should I be doing some of the searching, do you suppose? While irregular, it might not be quite so dreadful as if you were to be discovered in any of the women's rooms."

"But you won't know what you're looking for," he had explained to her when she had raised the idea previously.

"Neither do you, really. You'll just know it when you see it, isn't that right? Couldn't we say the same of me?"

"No, it is bad enough that you're involved at all, Caroline," he had forgotten himself in the moment and called her by her given name. It was a first for him. But he didn't retract it, just hurrying to cover the lapse.

"You cannot be the one to search. I assure you, your help in keeping watch is plenty important."

And so they had proceeded. Gilbert had found very little of note, just as she had predicted, in her father's room, where he had gone first. If anything, what little he had found only contributed to Mr. Smith's innocence rather than his guilt. He had been receiving correspondence from his clerks while here at Chester Hill. Many of them mentioned progress at his steam engine foundry. As Caroline had pointed out, if the man was profiting from the technology, why would he do anything to jeopardize it? It was disappointing but not terribly surprising at that point. Gilbert felt decidedly seedy searching his friends' rooms. Not that they were all bosom bows, of course, but after ten days together, they were very well acquainted. And searching their rooms felt like the lowest betrayal. Even if it was for noble reasons.

Gilbert was searching Mr. Browne's room while still keeping part of his focus on what might be happening in the hallway. He had finally come across something truly interesting, but now he could hardly breathe as he listened to Caroline.

"Oh, Mrs. Nesbitt, have you noted how darling this landscape is?"

Gilbert froze in the act of putting all the items in the drawer he had been rifling through back into their previous place. Caroline's overloud voice alerted him that they were no longer alone in that section of the house.

"What are you doing here by yourself, Miss Smith?"

The older woman had seemed very pleasant throughout the party, but Gilbert could hear judgment in her voice as she asked the question.

"Oh, I had to fetch something from my room and was arrested by the artwork. I haven't taken the time this week to appreciate them as I had meant to do."

Silence followed her words, and Gilbert could almost see the woman's frown even though he wasn't looking at them.

"You ought to be with the others, Miss Smith. As an unwed young woman, it isn't seemly that you be near the bedchambers unattended."

Outrage filled Gilbert at the thought of what Caroline must be feeling at hearing the older woman's judgemental tone. It had been exactly what she had feared.

"I appreciate your concern, Mrs. Nesbitt. I hadn't thought it would be questioned, since we've all been spending so much time together. But I will collect my maid to join me, as I am not quite finished enjoying the paintings. Or would you like to remain with me? It doesn't seem that you have had a chance to enjoy them either."

The older woman sniffed. "I have to return to my daughter."

"Of course. I shall rejoin you shortly."

Gilbert could hear the smile in Caroline's voice, and he marvelled at her ability to remain pleasant in the face of the older woman's treatment. He was only glad he had already tossed the Nesbitts' rooms. Imagine if the woman had found him there. He shuddered at the very thought.

There was a rustle of movement and the opening and shutting of doors. Gilbert supposed Caroline had returned to her chamber, ostensibly to fetch her maid. But Gilbert knew she had arranged for her maid to be occupied elsewhere. While Caroline trusted her servants, she didn't want the girl involved. Gilbert had respected that decision. The fewer people involved the better. And a young woman's lady's maid could have divided loyalties. Caroline's father paid her wages. Could she be trusted not to run to him with the information? Caroline hadn't wanted to test that question, and Gilbert had agreed with her. But now, she would have come in handy.

He remained as still as he could so as to not make a sound as he waited to see what would happen with the women. It was making him anxious though. There were still more rooms to search. And time was marching quickly by.

With relief he heard the shuffling walk of the large woman pass by the room he was in and then the beginning of her descent down the stairs. Gilbert marvelled at the fact that he hadn't noticed her arrival before Caroline had announced her. It should have been more obvious to him. He was clearly relying too heavily upon his unwilling partner. That would get them both in trouble.

"You can come out now," she whispered just loud enough for him to hear.

Gilbert quickly exited the Mr. Browne's room. "I found something that might be of interest, but I cannot take the time now to examine it," he whispered to her as he passed her by, gratified to see her eyes and smile widen equally.

He hurried into another room, trying to be as thorough but fast as possible. If Mrs. Nesbitt was already alerted to a situation, they might not have much time left.

His concern was justified about fifteen minutes later when Gilbert was in the last room he had left to search. His efforts had produced nothing. Frustration was welling in him. And then he froze.

"What are you doing still up here, Miss Smith, and without your maid?"

Mrs. Nesbitt's voice carried loudly throughout the tall ceilings of the hallway despite the rugs that usually stifled sound in the sleeping area of the large home.

Chapter Nineteen

C aroline was ready to sink through the floor. They were so close to being clear. But Mrs. Nesbitt hadn't come alone this time. She had a veritable pack of support with her. With a gulp she turned to smile at the approaching women.

"Oh good, Mrs. Nesbitt, you brought others to enjoy the artwork. I know you admonished me to come rejoin the group, but now that I am here enjoying the paintings, I just cannot seem to tear myself away."

"Why did you not have your maid join you, then, as I had also told you?"

Caro hoped her shrug appeared uncaring even though she was anything but. "She was otherwise occupied, and I did not intend to dally. I just couldn't help myself."

Lady St. John stepped past the other women who had varying stages of frowns upon their faces. "It is a remarkable collection and, no doubt, intended to be enjoyed. But the woman isn't wrong, my dear, you ought not be here on your own, so close to the bedchambers."

Fighting the blush that threatened to betray her anger and humiliation, Caroline tried to keep her smile in place. "You are quite right, my lady. I shall have to curtail my artistic appreciation for the time being." She turned to everyone else. "Do you wish to remain here or shall we return to our needlework?"

The other women appeared mollified by Caroline's apparent disregard for the attention. It was evident they were thinking she wouldn't be nearly so relaxed if there were something questionable afoot. There were several furtive glances shifting between Caroline and Mrs. Nesbitt, but most began to turn toward the stairs from which they came.

"Just one minute," Mrs. Nesbitt called out. "I don't believe you," she stated baldly. "We've been here for more than a week. If you were such a lover of paintings, why is it only today that you have taken it into your head to linger here so very long? No, I think there is something afoot."

"Something like what?" Caroline didn't mean to sound abrasive, but she couldn't allow that to pass.

"I'm not certain, but there's definitely something. My favorite hair clip has gone missing. I thought perhaps it fell behind the dresser, but mayhap you took it."

Caroline took a step back as though she had been physically attacked rather than verbally. Never, in all her days, had anyone accused her of anything underhanded, let alone thievery.

"You think I would steal your hair clip? But why?" It was a rash accusation and one that made no sense. As a very wealthy young woman she would have no need to take something that would so obviously be lesser quality than anything in her own possession. But she couldn't say that out loud, of course.

"I think everyone should check their belongings to make sure Miss Smith hasn't taken anything of theirs."

There was a murmur of disquiet amongst the gathered women while Caroline held her breath hoping someone would come to her defence. Lady St. John stood at her side but didn't say anything. Then someone said, almost apologetically, "Well, it couldn't hurt to check." And that's when Caro knew that everything was going to come to a crash. Because Gilbert was in that room. She only hoped he had found somewhere to hide. But if the lady was searching her own room, surely she would find him.

Closing her eyes for the briefest moment, Caroline thought to pray, but she wasn't certain this was the sort of thing He would listen to. She squared her shoulders and awaited her fate.

A shriek was heard, and then Lady Fanny came running back into the hallway, followed quickly by Gilbert Northcott. Suddenly pandemonium had broken loose. Caroline closed her eyes. Of all the rooms for Gilbert to be found in.

"Miss Smith, what is the meaning of this?" Mrs. Nesbitt demanded.

"Shouldn't you be asking Mr. Northcott that question?" she returned, trying to brazen it out.

"I am asking you," the other woman countered, her tone accusatory.

It was always the same. Life was so unfair. She would be ruined, and Northcott would get off without the least interference.

"I cannot fathom why you would ask me about Mr. Northcott's whereabouts. I was merely enjoying the paintings, as I told you. They are very involving."

"And you didn't notice a single gentleman hanging about?" Mrs. Nesbitt's sarcasm made it very evident that she didn't believe a word Caroline was saying to her. The other guests began murmuring and staring at her with speculative accusation shining bright in their eyes.

Gilbert heaved a heavy, dramatic sigh.

"Mrs. Nesbitt, you are forcing our hand. We were hoping to wait until we returned to Town to announce our happy news, but I cannot allow you to speak to my betrothed in such a way."

Gasps and titters filled the hallway as everyone present reacted to Gilbert's words. Caroline did her best not to react at all.

"Well," Mrs. Nesbitt sputtered. "Betrothed or not, you shouldn't be lurking about in hallways unchaperoned." She turned her glare back upon Caroline, perhaps even more angry than before. "And secrecy is an unsavory quality. Why ever would you keep such happy news to yourselves? You ought to allow the lot of us to rejoice with you."

Caroline blinked at this new attack, still reeling from Gilbert's announcement. She wanted to protest that it wasn't true, but there was no taking back such words. Lady St. John remained by her side, still without a word. Caroline's expression must have telegraphed something to the older woman because she suddenly came to life.

"Yes, yes, it is terribly exciting. The silly young people wished to savour their joy for a day or two before sharing it with everyone else. But now that their news is out, we will be sure to celebrate with them this evening. Now, let us all return to the salon. Lady Worth is surely wondering what has come of us and here luncheon is about to be served."

The rest of the group wandered away, even Mrs. Nesbitt, despite her dark mutterings and Lady Fanny's freezing glare. When the space was cleared of all but Gilbert, Caroline, and her chaperone, Lady St. John looked at the two of them assessingly.

"I know this is news to Caroline. I don't know what you were up to here, but it would seem that the two of you are now betrothed. We are going to return to the main floor, and the two of you will have five minutes to discuss matters in the yellow room with the door open. I will stand far enough away to provide you with a degree of privacy, but that is the best you're going to get. There will be no more scandalous behaviour on my watch. Am I clear?"

Despite the severity of her words, Caroline could see that there was a sparkle of something in the older woman's eyes. She wasn't sure if it was amusement or triumph or both. But it would seem that Lady St. John was not disappointed about the turn of events. Caroline wanted to crawl into a hole and die, but at least her chaperone was pleased.

She wasn't sure how she managed to make her legs carry her down the stairs as it felt, as though all the blood in her body had pooled in her feet and nothing seemed to work correctly. Caroline rather suspected that it was only Gilbert's hand on her elbow that kept her from crumpling into a puddle on the floor.

Before she was ready, she found herself in the bright, sunny yellow room staring out a window overlooking the lawns trying very hard not to be sick all over the lovely carpet spread upon the floor.

"I'm sorry, Caroline. I know it was a rash statement to make. But it was the only way to prevent your ruination. I had meant to rely upon my brother's assistance if this was to happen, but I just couldn't risk it. Please, say something."

They were standing as far from the open door as possible, and his voice was pitched so low Caroline almost had to lean toward him to hear him clearly, but still she felt the words all the way to her toes. He had done it for her. He might not have really wanted to make such a declaration, but he had done it to protect her. Her heart began to shiver with a longing for his love, and she tried to put a rein upon it but to no avail. It was good that he had proposed in order to protect her, she insisted to herself despite Lady Worth's previous words.

"What are you going to do about it, though, Mr. Northcott?" she too kept her voice low. "We cannot possibly be betrothed. You are investigating my father for something verging on treason."

"Well, as a matter of fact, I found enough evidence of your father's determination to continue working with his steam engine foundry that I can support your belief that he couldn't be involved."

Caroline was only slightly mollified. "But if there really is a threat against the railroads, we need to keep searching for the culprit, don't we?"

She wasn't sure what to make of his grin. "I wouldn't say no to your assistance, if you're offering it," Gilbert returned. "I haven't taken the time to examine it carefully, but I found a letter that might suggest that Mr. Browne is actually the one I was looking for. And just before Lady Fanny barged into her room, I found something incriminating there as well."

Caroline's jaw fell open in surprise. "Mr. Browne? I admit I find that difficult to believe. And Lady Fanny? Is *that* why she has been pursuing my father?"

"As we agreed, appearances can often be misleading."

Caroline gave her head a shake, recalling herself to why they were in the yellow room alone together.

"This is all well and good, Gilbert, but what about your rash declaration to Mrs. Nesbitt? Do you think to end the engagement after a suitable period of time?"

"End the engagement? That would hardly make this ordeal worthwhile, would it? I don't really see how that will prevent your ruination, do you?"

Caroline lifted her shoulder slightly. "That isn't really your problem to deal with, though, is it?"

"Would you have preferred me to say nothing and let that Nesbitt woman abuse you like she wanted?"

Caroline bit her lip, willing the tears to stay away, but her distress must have become evident as he suddenly put his arm around her. "Aw, no, Caro, please, don't cry. How can I fix this? I didn't think you cared overmuch who you married, as long as your father approved and you could tolerate the gent. I swear to you I'll be as tolerable as I can muster, if you'll have me. But if you truly wish to be free, I will try to figure out a way to undo what I've done."

Pulling out of his arm she peered up into his face to try and really understand what he was leaving unsaid. As she scoured his face with her gaze, he reached out gently and cupped her cheek in his hand. Her stomach fluttered in a much better way than it had been doing just moments before.

"Tell me what you're thinking," he whispered.

"I think you're going to regret it," she said immediately, surprised when he immediately shook his head.

"Only if you're unhappy about it," he said fiercely while still keeping his voice low. "I've loved having you partner with me in this venture. You already know the truth about my being an agent, so I don't need to keep secrets from you. And if you're willing or interested, we could stay partners in life and as agents."

Caroline's eyes widened, and she continued to search his face, seeing that he was serious. Her heart welled anew. But she sternly bade herself to remain calm.

"I don't want to love you," she whispered desolately.

"I didn't mean to love you, but it seems to have already happened for me," he answered her with a frown. "Can you tell me why you don't want to love me?"

Now her eyes nearly encompassed her whole head. "You love *me*?" she squeaked. He nodded but prodded her, "You didn't answer my question."

"Love ruined my mother's life."

"Do you think she thought that?"

Caroline again searched Gilbert's face before averting her gaze to the window. She offered a tiny shrug. "Maybe not. Perhaps it's more that my parents' love ruined my life."

Gilbert laughed a little. "Your poor life has been ruined rather frequently. But I can promise you that even if you were to find that you love me, it shan't ruin our children's lives. It might perhaps embarrass them, but they shall certainly have the most wonderful lives we can muster up for them, I can promise you that quite sincerely."

She brought her gaze back to tangle with his, a smile widening on her face. "You love me." She said it as though it were a dawning realization. She threw herself into his arms. "I love you, too."

His head was just lowering to seal their troth when there was the sound of a throat being cleared quite loudly near the door.

"I hesitate to interrupt such a moment, but I think you have quite compromised Caroline sufficiently for one day. I shan't allow you to be much more thorough in your efforts. I also happened to overhear a little of your conversation, and I have to say something that I should have said to Caroline long ago."

Caroline had jumped away from Gilbert when she'd heard the woman's voice, and she turned wide eyes upon Lady St. John, asking a question without words.

"Love did not ruin your mother's life. She was exceedingly happy until the day she died. None of us would have wished death for her, but I can assure you, many have envied the love your parents shared despite it being highly unfashionable. I am sure her family's reaction to your parents' marriage and subsequently toward you have not been enjoyable for you, but you cannot labour under the belief that it was your parents' love for one another that was at fault." Suddenly she turned her back on the two of them and left the room once more. "One more minute, and that's the end of it," Lady St. John called out with laughter sounding clearly in her tone.

Caroline stared at Gilbert. "Lady Worth said something similar," she admitted as a grin spread upon her face, and she actually jumped up and down. "Are you really going to make me an agent?" Caroline's voice dropped to a whisper, her eyes shining with delight, even as Gilbert pulled her back into his arms and his lips neared hers.

"We shall be the best team the Home Office has ever seen."

Her whoop of joy was muffled as his lips sealed over hers. They were going to have the best life ever.

Epilogue

G ilbert was frowning over a cryptic letter he had been sent when Caroline sailed into the room.

"I think you need to do something about Foster."

"And good morning to you, too, wife," he greeted drily, with a grin even as Caroline glided over and dropped a quick kiss onto his cheek. "What has Frost gotten up to now?"

"Daisy says he's tormenting her."

Gilbert finally looked up at his wife, a warm smile reflected in his gaze. "Torment is a rather strong word. Is that your description or Miss Alcott's?"

Caroline wrinkled her nose at him as she manoeuvred her increasingly cumbersome body onto his knee that he conveniently made available to her when he pushed back from his desk upon her approach.

"It might have been a combination of the two," she answered him with a grin. "Perhaps I was a bit rash when I suggested that we not go up to Town for the Season this year."

Gilbert settled his hand on her belly where their first child's movements were just beginning to be able to be felt.

"I think it might be a bit late for us to change our minds, my dear. And do you really think you would want to go about to events while you're increasing?"

Caro huffed a breath. "Well, not to balls or anything, but I could surely make calls. And more importantly I could receive calls, couldn't I? I could make sure your brother isn't making too much of a pest of himself."

"Do you really think Frost is pestering her? Or do you think perhaps it's something else entirely?"

Caroline's eyes widened as his meaning sank in, and she stood suddenly.

"I'll start packing immediately."

Gilbert watched his wife hurry from the room as fast as she was capable of doing while a grin stretched his face. Compromising his wife had been the best decision he'd ever made.

The End

- - - - - - - - - - - - - -

Want to find out what happens with Foster?
Read the next book in the *Northcott Kinship* series:

Evading the Gentleman

She doesn't want a love match, so why is her heart trying to convince her otherwise?

The *Northcott Kinship* series is connected to the *Sherton Sisters*. Have you read those yet?
Start with Book 1

A Duke to Elude

She's waiting for true love. He's tasked with uncovering the truth. When nefarious schemes threaten her reputation, he finds his heart on the line with it.

About the Author

I learned to read when I was four or five, listening to my mother read to me when I was lonely after my brother started school. Ever since, I've had my head buried in books. I love words – historical plaques, signs, the cereal box – but my first love has always been novels.

A little over ten years ago my husband dared me to write a book instead of always reading them. I didn't think I'd be able to do it, but to my surprise I love writing. Those early efforts eventually became my first published book – Tempting the Earl (published by Avalon Books in 2010). It has been a thrilling adventure as I learned to navigate the world of publishing.

I believe firmly that everyone deserves a happily ever after. I want my readers to be able to escape from the everyday for a little while and feel upbeat and refreshed when they get to the end of my books.

When not reading or writing, I can be found traipsing around my neighbourhood or travelling the world with my favourite companion.

Stay in touch:

Website   Facebook   Instagram   Twitter

Stay in touch with Wendy May Andrews
and forthcoming publishing news.

Sign up for her biweekly newsletter

Other books by Wendy May Andrews:

Ladies of Mayfair

The Governess' Debut

The Debutante Bride   The Reluctant Debutante

Sweet Surrender   A Dangerous Debut

Mayfair Mayhem

The Duke Conspiracy

The Countess Intrigue   The Viscount Deception

The Bequest

Inheriting Trouble

Courting Intrigue   Inviting Misfortune

Sherton Sisters

A Duke to Elude

A Viscount to Conspire   A Lady to Reveal

A Gentleman to Avoid   A Sister to Beguile

Northcott Kinship

Intriguing Lord Adelaide   Convincing Mr. Northcott

Orphan Train

Sophie

Cassie

Katie

Melanie

Proxy Brides

A Bride for Carter

A Bride for Ransom

A Bride for Alastair

A Bride for Hamilton

Dear Aunt Judy

Torn in Toronto

Singed in Saint John

If you like Regencies with a touch of adventure, you will love **the *Mayfair Mayhem* series. Book 1 is:**

The Duke Conspiracy

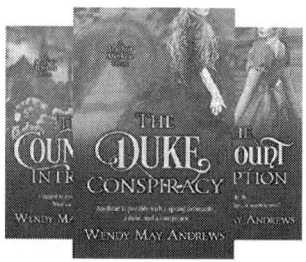

Anything is possible with a spying debutante, a duke, and a conspiracy.

Growing up, Rose and Alex were the best of friends until their families became embroiled in a feud. Now, the Season is throwing them into each other's company. Despite the spark of attraction they might feel for one another, they each want very different things in life, besides needing to support their own family's side in the dispute.

Miss Rosamund Smythe is finding the Season to be a dead bore after spying with her father, a baron diplomat, in Vienna. She wants more out of life than just being some nobleman's wife. When she overhears a plot to entrap Alex into a marriage of convenience, her intrigue and some last vestige of loyalty causes them to overcome the feud.

His Grace, Alexander Milton, the Duke of Wrentham, wants a quiet life with a "proper" wife after his tumultuous childhood. His parents had fought viciously, lied often, and Alex had hated it all.

Rose's meddling puts her in danger. Alex will have to leave the simple peace he craves to claim a love he never could have imagined. Can they claim their happily ever after despite the turmoil?

Available now on <u>Amazon</u>

If you like Sweet Regency Romance, read

A Duke to Elude

Book 1 in the *Sherton Sisters* series

She's waiting for true love.
He's tasked with uncovering the truth.
When nefarious schemes threaten her reputation, he
finds his heart on the line with it.

Lady Rosabel, eldest daughter of the Earl of Sherton, has no interest in being a Duchess, despite countless proposals from eligible nobility. Secretly, she is waiting for a love match—preferably with someone who carries no title. Bel's third Season is predictably disappointing until the mysterious Duke of Wexford arrives and has her questioning her plans to refuse any suitor with his status.

James Allingham, the 6th Duke of Wexford, seems to have inherited the role as advisor to the ailing King along with the dukedom. Investigating Lord Prescott's schemes is tricky enough without the interference of Lady Rosabel. She is beautiful and intelligent, but Wexford has no time for courting.

Wexford needs to uncover everything about Prescott's plans to destabilize the colonies. When Lady Rosabel is implicated in the schemes, James fights his suspicions of—and his attraction to—the beautiful young woman as he presses on to find the truth.

Discover the page-turning intrigue of this clean Regency romance today

Available now on <u>Amazon</u>

Made in the USA
Middletown, DE
15 April 2025

74308907R00135